STOLEN *at* SEA

Taken Series Book One

STOLEN
at SEA

Taken Series Book One

SUMMER O'TOOLE

Front cover image by Wander Aguiar Photography
Cover Model: Christoph L
Book design by Murphy Rae, www.murphyrae.com
Editing by Saxony Gray, Editing by Gray
Proofreading by Marissa Taylor
Formatting by Elaine York
www.allusionpublishing.com

Playlist

Save Me—Majk
Parallel Line—Keith Urban
Lie—Sasha Alex Sloan
Way down We Go—KALEO
My Thoughts On You—The Band CAMINO
Bitter—FLETCHER, Kito
Flames—R3HAB, ZAYN, Jungleboi
Paradise (feat. Dermot Kennedy)—MEDUZA,
Dermot Kennedy
Sunday—Joy Oladokun
Closer—Kings of Leon
Voodoo in My Blood—Massive Attack, Young Fathers
Miss Me—Jervis Campbell

And more...get the full playlist at
SummerOtoole.com/StolenAtSeaPlaylist

Dedicated to Grandma Chickie,
the matriarch of our family of strong women,
and who always has a book in her hand.

CHAPTER ONE

Date with Lord Barnaby Thomas

August 4, 1717
New Bern, Colony of North Carolina

He raced with such speed it seemed to defy the laws of nature. I forced myself not to blink for fear that I would lose track of his dashing and darting. He readied himself to make the jump from the branch of one oak tree to another ten feet away. My heart skipped a beat. Would he make it across safely?

It was too late now. His pursuer was hot on his tail, and this was his only route of escape. His body seemed to hang in midair, time slowed. Until at last, his body gripped tight to the trunk. *Landing successful.*

His pursuer hesitated at the end of the branch as if weighing the risks and rewards of taking the leap. The hesitation was all he needed, and my little friend scurried quickly out of sight, lost in the foliage.

"Nothing like them in the New World, I am most certain of it." Lord Barnaby Thomas's voice pulled my attention away from the squirrels.

"Like what, exactly?" I asked, looking back over his shoulder to see whether the pursuing squirrel had taken the jump. He was nowhere to be seen.

This wasn't the first time the squirrels in the grove of live oaks on Lord Thomas's expansive lawn—behind his even more expansive and impractically large house—had provided a mental escape from listening to him drone on about the most trivial and self-absorbed topics.

Over our month-long courtship, I'd been forced to listen to Lord Thomas talk about his favorite shirt not being ironed properly and his tea being served too hot to drink. The squirrels were a welcome respite. I envied how free and daring they were, leaping from limb to limb, no one telling them who to date and where to go. Unlike me, they didn't have parents pushing them toward a lord who was as drab as he was rich.

"Like these gems, of course." He looked at me like I had just made an exceptionally indecent remark, not a simple question.

In his hands was a jewelry box with the most outrageous necklace I had ever seen. A massive ruby that was set in gold and lined with diamonds hung in the center. Sapphires, emeralds and pearls were strung on either side of the ruby. I had most certainly never seen anything like it before. The sunlight made the colors even more vibrant. I raised my wine glass in a silent toast to their beauty and took a sip.

I was nearly twenty-three and still single, which to my mother was comparable to having a witch for a daughter. She was desperate to find me a husband, and much to my dismay, Lord Thomas was the one she settled on. When Lord Thomas first joined his parents in the colonies after he finished schooling in London, my mother kept arranging painfully obvious accidental run-ins.

First, she insisted I pick up her dress—that I had picked up the day before—from the tailor *again* and Lord Thomas just so happened to be picking up a suit at the same time. Next, she invited me to join her for tea with the ladies at the Thomas Estate. And what would you know, none of the ladies showed! Alas, it was just me and Lord Thomas after our mothers whisked away to another room in the house. After her third attempt, I had to intervene.

The conversation ended with me agreeing to a courtship with Lord Thomas for at least a month. If at the end of month, I was not smitten and engaged, my mother agreed to drop the issue and allow me to marry on my own time. Which brings me here, just four days away from the deadline, with about the same amount of affection for Lord Thomas as the local drunk.

"I, too, was quite speechless the first time I saw it." He sat up taller, adjusted his overly powdered wig and cleared his throat. "My lady, Sloane Patricia Sinclair."

My full name sounded foreign and patronizing in his crisp London accent, the King's English.

"Will you do me the honor of being my guest at tomorrow's Founder's Ball?"

Oh, how I wished I was a furry brown squirrel scampering about, my only concern remembering where I stashed my acorns. Instead, I was facing the threat of spending an entire evening with a man so horrifyingly boring and self-absorbed that he made me wish I was a squirrel.

"I would love nothing more," I said through gritted teeth, hoping my forced smile came off charming, and not like I was constipated. With the month almost up, I was hoping this would be our last date. But a promise is a promise and I agreed to say yes to every invitation during this seemingly endless month.

"Delightful! I'm sure the governor will be excited to have a *lord* attend his ball." I had to actively refrain from rolling my eyes. *Were all lords this obsessed with being lords?*

I didn't even know what he was lord of come to think of it. He must have told me, someone of his vanity surely wouldn't forget to mention *that,* but I could no better recall with a gun to my head. I had become so adept at letting his words float in one ear and out the other.

• • •

The steps to the grand front door were lined with lanterns that cast the tall columns in long shadows. Lord Thomas offered me the crook of his arm and I forced a smile as I linked mine with his.

Arm in arm, we followed behind another couple up the stairs. As we entered the main hall, two whispering women huddled together looked up at Lord Thomas. Their tight whispers turned into girlish giggles, and they teasingly waved their silk fans and ogled him with big doe eyes. *Oh, just what he needs,* more people fanning his giant ego.

"Well, I am pleased to see some people are still appreciative of being in the presence of a lord," he said, straightening his ascot. *This was going to be a very long night.*

I looked back at the women, still in a fit of giggles. *You can have him,* I wanted to shout at them.

Lord Thomas swiped two glasses of red wine from a passing servant's tray and handed one to me.

"Thank you, my lord."

"It's quite charming how quaint it is, really."

"What is, my lord?" I asked as I scanned the room trying to see what he was talking about. Groups of young couples chatted animatedly with each other and bright colors swirled in the center of the room where pairs danced, the ladies' dresses ranging from crimson to gold to bright emerald. A quartet played pleasingly, not too slow but not too fast, perfect for dancing. Servers dressed smartly in black & white circulated around the room with trays of food and drink.

This was easily one of the nicest gatherings I had ever attended. What with the high ceilings lined with golden trim and three giant crystal chandeliers lighting up the room. I honestly had no idea what Lord Thomas was referring to. I wouldn't describe anything in this room as "quaint."

"Just how the nouveau riche attempts to keep up with the ton. Folks here have a few successful harvests, or whatever it is you people do, and think they are kings and queens." He let out a hearty laugh dripping with condescension. I wanted to throw my glass of wine at his ridiculously impractical white silk vest.

"*These* people work hard for everything they own. Many of them came to the New World with nothing but the clothes on their backs and made a place for themselves—like my father." He looked at me, slightly taken aback by my raised voice. "Maybe you find it quaint because you've never had to break a sweat in your life, have slaves and servants to do everything for you—do they wipe your arse too?—and have been handed everything on a damn golden platter?" He looked around to see if my little spat had attracted anyone's attention.

"Well, aren't you in a fiery mood tonight?" He patted me on the shoulder and steered me away from the center of the room, ushering me away from the curious eyes leering our way. "Your passion is one of the things I adore most about you," he said loudly enough for eavesdroppers to hear, as if to assure others he was in on the joke. Once out of earshot of others, he hissed in my ear through the gritted teeth of a forced smile, "Your hysterical outburst is causing people to stare."

"I thought you enjoyed the attention, *my lord*." I stepped out of his grasp and crossed the hall to an open window. It was suffocating being around someone so obsessed with others' opinions and so detached from the real world. I let the cool, fresh air wash over me and took a few deep breaths.

Maybe if I wasn't at the ball with Lord Thomas to placate my mother's obsession with marrying me off, I could have met someone tonight who didn't make me want to rip out all my hair. But surely my mother doesn't care about what I actually want in a life partner.

My shoulders tightened as I heard the lord's nasally voice approaching me from behind.

"My lady, I'd like to introduce Mr. Clayton McCabe." I turned around and offered a small curtsy to a young man with a wig sitting slightly askew on his head and his jacket buttoned off by one.

"It's my pleasure to make your acquaintance, Mistress Sloane." He slurred his words so the last two sounded more like "Miss Tiss Slow." *Well, perhaps this drunkard will be more entertaining than Lord Thomas.*

"Lord Thomas tells me you like to play shopkeeper."

"Play shopkeeper?" I asked.

"Oh, yes, you know how little girls play house, pretending to cook and clean and mother and such? Well, you like to pretend to be a businesswoman." He and Lord Thomas both howled.

"I don't pretend to be anything, Mr. McCabe." My icy tone instantly put a stop to their laughing. "I am a businesswoman, and I am damn good at it, too. I've been working alongside my father since I was knee-high, and I do not appreciate you mocking me or my family's business with your ignorance."

McCabe's mouth gaped open, and his thick whiskey breath assaulted my senses.

"And do close your mouth before you start catching flies, sir." I began to walk away, but his hand wrapped around my bicep and yanked me back.

"You stuck-up hag! How dare you speak to me like that?" his face contorted in rage.

Why was it that men always expected women to take their rude comments as a compliment? McCabe was far from the first man to become enraged when all I did was stand up for myself. But I wouldn't lower myself to his level by lashing back in a shouting match. No matter how badly I wanted to.

"Kindly remove your hand, Mr. McCabe. Apparently, my sweet rose has thorns."

The lord chuckled awkwardly, clearly uncomfortable with the conflict. *Classic Baby-Hands Barney.* A nickname inspired by my father when he remarked how soft Lord Thomas's hands were after the first time they met. If there was one sure-fire way to lose my father's respect, it was men whose hands weren't callused from hard, honorable work.

"You may want to let go, lest you get pricked," Lord Thomas said. His nervous laughter continued. Was he really more concerned with diffusing McCabe's anger than defending me?

"I can speak for myself, lord." I looked McCabe in the eyes and said calmly, "Take your hands off me. And if you ever lay a hand on me again, you will regret it."

McCabe huffed before releasing his grip and stomping away like a spoiled child who was slapped on the wrist.

"I am leaving, and I am taking the carriage," I said to Lord Thomas, who was still muttering something about roses and thorns. "Perhaps you can catch a ride home with your new friend." I turned and left, leaving him standing there stunned by the first rejection he'd probably ever received.

I silently seethed while waiting for the carriage to be brought around. Part of me wanted to storm back in and yell at the lord for discrediting my capabilities, not defending me, and then, after all that, having the gall to try to speak for me when McCabe grabbed me. *He created the problem and then wanted to solve it?* No, thank you. I can fight my own fights.

The carriage arrived and I opened the door and climbed in before the coachman could even get up from the reins. I was eager to get away from this idiotic ball filled with idiotic men.

The ride home was quiet without Lord Thomas chattering incessantly like a crow. Listening to the cicadas and the sound of trotting hooves calmed me down. There was always something about the nighttime symphony that I found comforting and soothing, no matter how riled up I was.

My father wasn't an angry man, but on the infrequent occasions when something got under his skin, he really lit up. There was no doubt I got my temper from him. You could stab my mother and she'd still probably smile while offering you a biscuit.

I had the coach drop me off at the start of our property. With the recent rain, the uphill road to our house turned into a muddy slope, impossible for carriage wheels to get traction.

As I approached the house, I spotted my parents sitting on the porch, as they did most nights, a whiskey in hand. My mother always stayed in her elegant day dresses until she was turning in for the night. Never slipping on a night robe to read by the fire or a more comfortable homespun for dinner with just me and my father. In fact, I never saw her out of her bedroom in her night robe. My father on the other hand, grew up a cotter's son in Scotland and couldn't stand to stay in his respectable stiff jacket and wig longer than absolutely necessary. Dressed in only his breeches and stockings, long shirt untucked and wig off, he looked like a farmhand stealing sweet moments with the mistress of the house.

I heard my name in conversation and paused unseen under the cover of an oak tree to listen.

"Business is no place for a woman of her age. You're only getting her hopes up, John." It was a sentiment my mother voiced often. I rolled my eyes in the dark and felt a familiar feeling of frustration build in my chest.

"She's good at it, Beatrice." My cheeks flushed at my father's praise. "She's canny and has a good head for numbers. If she was a son, rather than a daughter, her place at the head of the company would never be in doubt. I don't see what difference her wearing a dress rather than breeks makes."

"Oh please, John, it's not about how she dresses."

"So, ye're saying yer mind wouldn't be altered if she replaced her lace skirts for tweed trousers?"

"Stop that." I could hear my mother laugh, despite her strong feelings on the matter. "You know as well as I do that just because we see the strong, witty woman she is, doesn't mean others will too."

I could sense my father's sigh, knowing her words were true. Oh, how I wanted him to tell her she was wrong, that I was the perfect fit.

"But if she had a husband," she continued, "he could be the face of the business dealings and she could still be intimately involved behind closed doors."

"And what do ye propose we do about that? Purchase an advertisement with the printer? *Seeking husband to run family business but only publicly, wife will run all other dealings privately.*"

"No. We simply stop allowing her to pursue this foolish fantasy."

Foolish fantasy? What was foolish was wasting my life only hosting tea parties and changing clouts! I had heard enough, I stepped out from under the oak tree. My parents' conversation halted as soon as they saw me.

Why did I have to give up on my dreams just to become someone's wife? Just to be pushed to the sidelines and cast in the shadow of a husband. It's not like I wanted to run away and join the circus. I wanted to contribute to our family business, continue to grow the Sinclair legacy.

"You're home early," my mother said as I climbed the porch steps. "How was the ball?"

"A real-life fairytale." I groaned before kissing them both on the cheek and wishing them a goodnight. The evening ended much sooner than expected, but I was still exhausted and headed straight to bed.

I paused before walking inside. "Meet you at the warehouse tomorrow?"

"O'course, my girl," said my father. *At least I had that to look forward to.*

CHAPTER TWO

No Small Promise

When I woke the next morning, the sky was a brilliant blue and the summer rainstorms left everything green and lush. Humidity hung in the air carrying with it the subtle smells of the river and wet earth.

The local birds made their presence known, filling the morning with their songs. It was said that birds used their songs to communicate, but I always wondered how effective it was when they all sang over each other. I crossed the dewy lawn to the stables behind the house.

We had grooms to look after our horses, but I always tended to Gerty, my buckskin horse, myself. She was born to one of our mares when I was ten. My father had wanted to sell her, and she would have fetched good money, but I begged my father to let me keep her.

My father permitted me to keep her but under one condition—I care for her completely by myself to teach me responsibility and ownership. His favorite saying was "if you want something done right, do it yourself."

Gerty was a sweet foal, with giant ears and knobby knees, she had two moods—jumping like a rabbit, kicking her legs in the air, or sleeping with her head in my lap. When she was just a week old, her mother died from birth complications. My father didn't let that change our deal: no one was allowed to help me bottle feed her every three hours in the absence of her mother, but I didn't mind much.

God, I loved that spindly little horse so much. I would spend many nights sleeping in her stable, both of us curled up on the hay together until she would wake me by nipping at my hair to let me know she was hungry.

I opened the big barn doors, Gerty whinnied from her stall and my heart lightened at the sound. The earthy and moist smell of the stables always felt like coming home.

"Hey, girl." I stroked her long nose in greeting As I brushed and saddled her, I began to tell her about my evening and the lord's theatrics. "He starts off by insulting basically everyone in the room, calling us the 'nouveau riche.'"

Gerty stomped her foot in disapproval as she blew a puff of air out her nose.

"My thoughts exactly! Yet, the whole time women were practically drooling over him. I don't get it." I led her by the reins across the stable floor to the door. "What can they possibly see in him?"

She neighed and shook her head.

"His family may be the richest in the colony, but you couldn't pay me enough to spend a single second more with him after this month is up."

She huffed in agreement.

"And don't even get me started on this McCabe figure—but that's a story for another time, we got places to be." I kissed her fuzzy pink nose. "Thanks for listening, Gert." I jumped on her back, and she took off riding to the warehouse, a mile away into town.

Our warehouse was the biggest building on the block. Previously old storage for the military, it was one of the older buildings in New Bern and it showed. The siding was natural wood, bleached and dry from years exposed without paint. My mother always wanted my father to paint it, but he refused, saying it gave the building character. I agreed: the wood, despite being worn down and rugged compared to some of the new buildings, still stood strong. It weathered hurricanes and blizzards but was never knocked down.

I hobbled Gerty near a public trough and a small clearing of grass across the street. I was always proud to look across the street and see our name painted in big, bold letters on the front, *Sinclair Trading Co.* It was the only paint on the building, a concession my father was happy to make.

My father and his twin brother immigrated to the colonies when they were just fourteen years old after their parents died of the pox. With nothing but the clothes on their backs, the two orphans talked their way onto a ship as galley boys. It was the hardest job he'd ever had. Which really said something as he worked as a cooper assistant, farm hand and logger all before setting sail.

The trading company was actually an idea he and his brother came up with on their overseas journey. There was a rich merchant on board with them who was the only person other than the captain to have his own quarters, who got extra rations and never was called to work when they were short-handed. He didn't seem to struggle or want for anything and that level of stability to two orphan boys was very appealing.

They would be starting from zero, no fancy ships or connections in every port like the wealthy merchant. But they did estimate they would have earned just enough coin at the end of the voyage to buy themselves a donkey. And with a donkey, they could travel between towns, their ass loaded with goods to trade.

My father and his brother were cleaning the deck one day when a cannon ball blew through the wood siding. The force knocked my father off his feet and his head hit the deck, losing consciousness. When he woke minutes later, his body like a pin cushion of wood shrapnel, the ship had already been boarded by pirates.

Pirates and crew fought bloodily, the air thick with gunpowder smoke and men rushing in every direction. It was chaos and violence like he'd never seen before.

And next to him lay his twin brother, his only remaining family, dead with a large spear of wood protruding from his neck. I only heard the story once and once was enough. The pain in my father's eyes when he told me about his brother was so unbearable, I never wanted to see him like that again.

The brave, little man that he was reached the New World and used all his coin to buy an old but sturdy mule. Sinclair Trading Co. was born, a brokerage between the backcountry and the port cities.

The company became so much more than just a means of making a living: It was a promise kept to a lost brother.

Since I was wee, I was my father's shadow as he continued to grow the company into a successful and well-respected business in the colonies. We'd take trips to the backcountry to buy goods from the homesteaders camping along the route under the stars. He taught me how to keep a ledger and drive a hard bargain.

I think in some way, I was trying to fill the hole that his brother's death left.

This morning, my father was standing out front, his back to me, staring up at the large painted letters. I often would catch him in moments like this and wonder if he was imagining it read "Sinclair Brothers Trading" instead. I never had the heart to ask him if that was the case. Mostly, because I feared I'd be right and that I wasn't enough to fill that void, no matter how hard I tried.

"Morning," I said. He turned and waved, a warm smile across his face. "What's on the agenda for today?"

"A potential vendor is coming in, a bee keep. Said in his letter he's got honey and wax."

"Just beeswax, or has he made candles or soap out of it?" I asked.

"We'll have to wait and see. In the meantime, come help me with stock for our trip inland. Malcolm should be back tomorrow, if not the next day."

Malcolm was my best friend Abigail's husband. Abigail and I grew up together, she was the closest thing I'd ever had to a sibling. Practically a part of our family, when she married, my father offered her new husband a job with the company making regular trips to the backcountry for goods.

He was good people. Abigail loved him and he treated her well. He was trustworthy and reliable in the employment of the Sinclair Trading Co. So, when my father needed someone to send to France on his behalf to oversee an important shipment, Malcolm was a natural choice.

My father was in the back office while I was out front on the warehouse floor when a man walked in. He paused just inside the doorway, looking around at the dozens of barrels, crates and linen-wrapped bundles of stock.

"Good morning, sir. What can I help you with?" he started as if spooked by my voice. I suppose he hadn't seen me among all the goods.

"Good day to ye, miss. I'm looking for Mr. John Sinclair."

"He's occupied at the moment, but I'm his daughter and would be more than happy to assist."

He dropped the rucksack that he'd been carrying, making a small plume of dust. He was about my father's age, dressed in a nice jacket and shirt that were well worn, probably his only dress clothes for important occasions.

"No, no," he said, "I'll be waiting for Mr. Sinclair himself."

"I'm certain I can help you just the same. Do you want to show me your wares and we can discuss pricing?"

He scoffed. "I'll no' be letting a woman settle the price for me—What do you know 'bout business?" *God, was there something in the water?* What was with all these men treating me like a silly little girl who can barely count to ten?

"Sir, I will price them the same as my father. But if that's not good enough for you, you're welcome to leave." I pointed at the door he'd just come through. At that moment, my father walked out and Mr. I-Belittle-Women eagerly turned to him.

"Ah, good, Mr. Sinclair, a pleasure to meet ye. I'm Mr. Abraham Long," he hurriedly approached him, hand outstretched. "We were just waiting for ye."

My father shook his hand but didn't smile.

"Did my daughter not offer to help ye?" My father wasn't a big or burly man, but he stood tall and carried a proud and unshakable air about him, Mr. Long seemed to shrink in his presence.

"Uh, no, sir er—Well yes, I suppose she did."

"Good, then I'm sure ye'll be eager to show her what ye've brought with ye today." Mr. Long stuttered in his response and my father left the same way he came but not without giving me a slight wink. He always had my back.

• • •

It didn't take long to settle a deal. Long's honey was thick and cream-colored with plenty of crystallization and few pollen particles—high quality. His tapered beeswax candles were also nicely done with even size and shape. It was an easy buy and after his previous behavior, he didn't dare try to haggle too much.

Once he left, I went to see my father in his office. Boxes piled up in every corner and a crooked stack of ledgers piled next to his desk. The desk itself was covered in a mix of tea mugs, yesterday's lunch dishes and several broken quills. My mother would have a fit if she was to see the state of his office.

"Dear lord, Da." I instantly began gathering dishes and sorting papers. "Are you planning on hibernating here for the winter?"

"Don't tell yer mother." He chuckled.

In my tidying, I uncovered the loan note for the wine order. A reminder that the trip to France Malcolm was on wasn't just important, it was everything.

For decades, the family business dealt solely in colony produced goods. They didn't require certificates or approval from the Crown to trade and sell. And my father made quite a profitable business from this inventory alone, but he always wanted to expand. So, when Lord Thomas mentioned his cousin was getting married and looking for quality French wine to serve, I immediately knew this was my chance to prove to my family that I deserved my spot as the head of the business.

I brought the proposal to my father, and he loved the idea, especially since we already would have a major client lined up. Now that he was a respected and influential figure in trade, he was able to receive approval from the Crown to begin selling taxed and regulated goods. Making him the first and only legal distributor of imported wine and liquor in the colony of North Carolina and her bordering colonies.

My parents invested a lot of their own savings into the shipment, but also took out a loan against our warehouse—and all the goods in it—to pay the full amount. It sounded like high stakes, having our business on the line, but once the Thomases purchased their portion of the wine for the wedding, we would pay off the loan immediately. I couldn't help thinking of all the affluent wedding guests who would quickly learn of our new stock too. Things were about to really change for us.

"How was last night?" my father asked as I finished straightening up his files.

I groaned. "Well, the lord seemed to think he was doing us peasants a great honor by gracing us with his presence." My father laughed. "And I left early after a small row over our difference of...*perspective*." No use in going into detail. My father already knew the kind of man Lord Thomas was.

"I appreciate ye puttin' up with that buffoon for your mother's sake, Sloane."

"She runs a tight ship." We both laughed at the truth in that. "But you promise, Da, to let me ultimately choose who I marry after this?"

"I promise, my girl." He cupped my cheek sweetly. "I learned a long time ago that it's a losing game trying to make ye do something ye dinna want to do."

I smiled back, knowing that a promise from my father was a guarantee. The oath of a Scottish man was solid as stone.

CHAPTER THREE

The Wine Shipment

I squeezed Abigail's hand at the first sight of the *Lilliana's* helm and mast as it revealed herself coming around the river's bend. We had been waiting along the river all morning. Watching the water for the ship felt like watching a candle slowly melt. Abigail had been anxiously pacing back and forth, her heels a constant tapping on the cobblestone. She started every sentence with "What if..." and then trailed off into her own thoughts. I tried to be reassuring and comforting, but I was just as anxious, though for different reasons.

While I was preoccupied with the wine venture's imminent success, I knew Abigail was wondering if her husband would be walking off the ship into her arms or if the captain would meet her with his condolences.

Long journeys on land were dangerous enough, but long journeys overseas were a straight up gamble. Between storms, disease and pirates, there was a strong likelihood Malcolm would not be returning home today.

I grabbed both her hands and made her look at me. "Abigail, listen to me." Her hands were shaking in mine. "Malcolm is going to come running off that ship and whisk you away and won't let you leave the house all weekend, alright?"

"Okay, but what if—" her voice cracked, and her eyes were glossy with tears.

"What if nothing—look it's getting closer."

The small ship in the distance grew bigger and bigger, until finally the giant transatlantic cargo ship towered above us as it docked.

As soon as the first sailor stumbled down the gangway, I knew something wasn't right. The men disembarking were worse for wear, but alive and walking. It was when men started being carried off on boards or draped around another mate's shoulder, that we realized not only was something not right, but something was terribly wrong.

It felt like the wind was knocked out of me. Abigail kept trying to push through the crowd, searching every face for her husband. I heard my father's voice boom asking what had happened. Two bodies covered with a sheet were carried down and Abigail tugged on my sleeve.

"I can't, Sloane, will you look? Will you see if it's M-m-m—" she couldn't finish saying his name, a sob choking her. I gave her a nod, my own throat getting tight.

"May I?" I asked one of the men carrying the pallet with the bodies. He made an affirmative grunt, it seemed everyone was having trouble getting their words out. My heart pounded sickeningly fast as I lifted up the corner of the sheet.

The faces staring back at me were swollen and bruised, dried blood matted their hair and streaked their dirty shirts. Though it was hard to distinguish features through the damage, I knew neither was Malcolm by their dark hair.

"It's not him," I said to Abigail, the tension in her shoulders releasing slightly. But instantly, we began scanning the disembarking crew again for Malcolm.

Finally, a familiar strawberry-blond head popped out at us. At the sight of her husband, Abigail barreled through the crowd with shocking vigor for such a petite woman, tears staining her cheeks.

He was conscious, which was better than some of the crew, but he was barely able to carry his own weight. His feet dragged limply while he hung between two sailors, his arms hooked around their necks. His face was battered but not too concerning. It was his abdomen that ripped the air from my lungs.

His shirt was flayed open, and a deadly-looking gash scored from just under his right rib to left hip. There was so much blood. His eyes seemed to be fluttering, barely staying open. But when he saw Abigail, they widened and lit up. "My sweet, Abby," he sighed with a slight upturned smile before promptly losing consciousness.

"What the hell happened?!" I demanded of the two men holding up Malcolm.

"Pirates, milady."

• • •

The whiskey glass shattered against the wall, rocking the Scottish landscape painting hanging there. My mother rolled her eyes in exasperation and flopped onto the parlor couch.

"They will burn in hell!" My father's face roared red, his hand that had thrown the glass still shaking. "Those bloody bastards will take everything from me! I shoulda gone myself. If ye want something done right, ye have to do it yerself."

"There's nothing you could have done, John," my mom repeated for the hundredth time that evening. "What were you going to do? Fight an entire pirate crew off single-handedly?!"

"First my twin brother,"—his voice caught in his throat—"and now our lives' savings, gone. Not to mention the fact we'll lose the entire company if we can't pay back the loan and the wedding is in less than a month." He reached for my mother's unfinished drink resting on the side table and I braced for impact, but he only took a large sip and collapsed onto the couch next to my mother.

My mother's words were true, there was nothing anyone could have done to prevent the shipment from being stolen. Once the pirates had decided to board the ship, the wine and brandy were as good as gone. But I couldn't stop feeling like it was all my fault. Guilt and anxiety gnawed at me.

I had insisted that this venture was the next tier of success for the Sinclair Trading Company. I had encouraged my parents to dump the massive amount of funds into this false promise. How could I be so reckless? There had to be something I could do to fix this utter disaster I had created.

My mind spun madly. Every time I tried to think of ways to dig us out of this pit, my thoughts would just go right back to my ever-growing guilt. I couldn't focus on anything other than how I had destroyed our family and our legacy with one foolish idea.

A knock came from our front door and all three of us were on our feet in a second. Was it news of the pirates? The wine, did the authorities recover it?

My father left the parlor to open the door and a few moments later returned with Lord Thomas in tow. What in God's name was *he* doing here?

"My dear Sloane and Mrs. Sinclair." He made a show of bowing slowly and kissing my mother's hand and then mine. I quickly yanked it back and looked at him daringly.

"What are you doing here, my lord?" I didn't even care that my tone did nothing to hide my annoyance with his surprise visit. My mother shot me a look from the corner of her eyes that I knew well. W*atch your manners.*

"Well, Mr. and Mrs. Sinclair," he addressed my parents, but avoided eye contact with my father; he seemed to be intimidated by anyone with a backbone. "I heard what happened at the dock today." He leaned closer to them and whispered like it was scandalous gossip, "You know, with the wine?"

"Of course, we know about the wine. Get on with it." My father's voice was so stern and cold I thought Baby-Hands Barney would run out the door.

"Um, yes, very well." He cleared his throat. "I would like to ask for your blessing to marry your daughter. As her husband, I would be delighted to provide any resources necessary to rebuild the good name of the Sinclair Trading Company."

My initial reaction was to laugh. But then I realized he was serious, and my hands started to sweat and my stomach sunk. My mother's eyes grew wide, and she started fanning herself obnoxiously. With the lord's money and influence, we could easily recoup the loss and set the business back on a safe and profitable path. I could see it in her face that this was a nightmare turned into a dream. Not only would our business be saved, but I would also finally be engaged to Lord Thomas. I felt sick realizing that it really was our best option at this point.

Any hope of leading the family business would be a mere memory of a wishful fantasy. Not to mention the simple fact that I could not stand the man.

I was not naive enough to think that people never married for convenience or reasons outside of love. But I also wasn't desperate enough to think that a loveless marriage was the best I could do. It's not that I didn't want a husband; I didn't want a husband to replace me.

I would die before I let Lord Thomas whisk in here and put a pretty bandage over a mess that was my responsibility to clean up. If I married him now, I would forever be the reckless daughter who nearly lost the company, and he would be the heroic lord saving the day.

But then I remembered the promise my father made me. Just yesterday, he swore to me that I would get to choose who I married. So, while the pressure was on, this wasn't a done deal. Surely my father would not give his blessing without my approval. And I would get that wine back, come hell or high water, before I said yes to anything Lord Thomas was offering.

"My Lord, what glorious news! John, your blessing?"

My mother looked at my father expectantly. Yet, I felt calmer in that moment than I had all day, knowing his blessing would never be given. My father's jaw was clenched and his chin held high.

"O' course, Lord Thomas, it would be an honor to have ye as my daughter's husband."

"What!" My chest felt like it was going to break into a thousand pieces. "Father, but—"

"I have made my decision." His voice was even and firm, but his eyes reminded me of the way they looked when he told me about his brother's death. Hollow and aching. *Why are you doing this!?* I tried to scream at him with my stare as Lord Thomas turned his attention to me.

"So, I guess all that is left is one question—Will you marry me, Sloane?" It seemed like everyone in the room held their breath at the same time. I didn't know what to do, I couldn't say no, but I couldn't say yes either. I needed time.

Time to figure out where those bloody pirates were and how I was going to get my wine from them. The enormity of the situation was like a block of iron on my chest. All I had to do was hunt down murdering, thieving pirates and somehow take back a ship full of wine. *No problem, that shouldn't be hard at all!*

Time, Sloane, you need more time. Focus.

"My lord, I am flattered by your proposal, but I am feeling faint from the day's events. I best lie down for the night. We'll continue this conversation tomorrow?"

"Certainly, sleep well—" Before he even finished his thought, I was already leaving the room.

I rushed up the stairs to my bedroom. I grabbed my cloak off a hook by my door, locked the door and went straight to the window across the room.

It would be a cold day in hell when I would marry Sir Barnaby Thomas, Lord of God-Knows-What. I had put my family in this mess, and I was going to fix it.

I sat on the open windowsill and looked down at the grassy ground below. I hadn't made this jump in many years. I used to sneak out my window to the stables at night, my mother thinking I was tucked soft and sweet into bed. On clear nights, the moon was bright enough for a starlit ride. I loved the chorus of insect noises at night punctuated by owl hoots and rustling leaves in the wind. It reminded me of nights on the road with my father.

Before I could change my mind, I pushed myself out the window. The soft grass cushioned my fall and then just like old times, I made my way under the moonlight to the stables.

CHAPTER FOUR

The Mutiny

"Sloane?" Abigail opened the door, rightfully surprised to see me on her doorstep. "What are you doing out here? Sneakin' round like a thief in the night!" She hustled me inside.

"How is Malcolm? I need to speak with him."

"He's awake but weak." She looked at me curiously. I hurried past her to the back corner of their small, one-room cabin where their bed was nestled against the wall. Homely aromas of broth wafted from the pot over the fire and a single lit taper candle cast the space in a soft, warm, glow. It could have been any other night if it wasn't for the pile of bloody rags and linens on the floor next to the bed.

I knelt beside the bed and took Malcolm's clammy hand in mine. He turned, and I was surprised to find his cheeks still had hints of rose instead of the pale white I was expecting.

"How are you?" My eyebrows knitted together as I glanced toward his torso, wrapped in layer upon layer of cloth, yet crimson blood still seeped through. The fact that he made it off the boat alive was a hopeful sign. The blade must not have cut anything vital, or he would have bled out long before reaching the harbor.

"Just a wee scratch." He cracked a sideways smile.

"The surgeon said no organs were damaged by some miracle, just a flesh wound really for all the gore." Abigail came up behind me. "He'll look like a butcher's block for the rest of his life with a scar like that, but he'll be just fine." The way she said *just fine* was taut with relief and love.

Relieved as I was too, I was there for a reason. "Mac, what happened with the pirates?"

"They weren't no pirates." He took a deep breath and winced at the slight movement. "It was mutiny."

"What do you mean, among your crew?" I asked.

"We were only a few hours away from the mouth of the Neuse, when we saw a military ship flying English colors. They were signaling for help, so we came about broadside. That's when they attacked." He fell silent, his gaze distant as if he was recalling that moment again.

"What then?" Abigail encouraged him to continue, soft hand on his shoulder.

"None of our crew was prepared for a fight, we weren't expecting it...it was a slaughter."

"I'm so sorry, Malcolm." I was responsible for his trauma too. He lay cut open like a deer, alive by some miracle.

"Nothing you could have done. There was no way to know what was going to happen." Abigail saw the tears brimming my eyes and tried to reassure me. She was too kind of a person. She nearly lost her husband and here she was comforting me.

"She's right, Sloane. This isn't your fault." His green eyes looked up at me with no hint of resentment or anger. I was lucky to have such forgiving people in my life. "Let me tell you the rest of what I know."

"Tell me, thank you."

"Once I was cut, I somehow managed to stumble my way to a storage closet. It was small and had nothing of value in it to the raiders, thought it would be a good place to hide. But when I went in, there was one of the raiders already inside. He was young and gangly, didn't look the fighting type. In fact, he looked more terrified of me than I was of him.

"We hid together while the raiders transferred over barrels of Mr. Sinclair's wine and the other cargo. While we waited, he told me about the mutiny."

"Do you trust him to be telling the truth?"

"I do, he was trying to escape from his crew, see. That's why he was in the closet hiding." Abigail got up to tend to the soup, while Malcolm told me what the man had shared.

It was indeed an English military ship, but half the crew were convicts pressed to service. Taken from their home country and forced to work in terrible conditions with no pay since they were still prisoners. Their resentment was a spark that quickly spread like a wildfire. Until it burned the captain, or more literally, threw him into the ocean wrapped in chains and cannon balls.

The crew members thought they could make much more committing piracy on unsuspecting trade ships. Given that they were already criminals, they didn't have anything to lose.

Then they could return to shore safely, but not as a mutinous gang of prisoners, but as loyal agents of the Crown who tragically lost their beloved captain. I couldn't help but feel hatred for the greedy men who turned their back on their own crew for the blood-soaked riches of high-sea piracy. At the expense of the life and livelihood of honest men like my father, Malcolm, and everyone else on the ship from France.

"Why was the man in the closet trying to escape? Was he not part of the mutiny too?" I asked.

"He was against the mutiny but remained silent. The new captain was killing anyone who protested. He figured the best way to stay alive was to keep his mouth shut until he had a chance to get off the ship. He was one of the men who helped carry me off the ship." It felt like a lifetime ago, watching Malcolm's bloody body being dragged down the gangway. *Was that really just this morning?* So much had changed so quickly.

"You said the mutineers were planning on returning to shore as innocent soldiers, do you know where?" A spark of a plan was forming in my head.

"He said they were going to anchor off the coast of Beaufort, they didn't want to risk getting blocked in on the river." Malcolm's words made me jump to my feet with excitement.

"Oh, Mac, that is just the best news—thank you!" I wrapped Abigail in a hug before kissing Malcolm on the forehead.

Abigail stopped me at the door. "And just where in God's name are you going?!"

"Beaufort."

"Are you bloody mad, woman?" Abigail was used to putting up with my shenanigans in the many years we'd been friends, so I knew she was only pretending to be shocked.

"Most likely."

"Sloane." She physically blocked my path by standing in front of the door. "I know this shipment was important to you, but what exactly are you planning to do?"

"The bastards are going to come ashore high and mighty thinking they have fooled everyone. Like Malcolm said, they'll pretend they are just regular old soldiers on land and pirates at sea. They think they can have the best of both worlds. But I won't let them."

"How?" she asked.

"There's a small garrison in Beaufort. I've been there a dozen times with my father and know the town well. I'm going to tell the garrison's colonel everything Malcolm just told me. And it won't be hard to convince him, all the proof I need is on the ship."

"Okay, but why not wait until morning and go with your father?" she whispered as Malcolm had started snoring, apparently having fallen asleep.

"I can't risk waiting too long and letting them sail away. Plus, if I don't get the wine back soon...I'll have to marry Lord Thomas."

"What!" she nearly shouted, her eyes wide in disbelief.

"He came over just now and proposed, implying that if I accepted, he could buy us a whole new shipment of wine and pay off our loan. My parents insisted it was the only way to fix this, even my father." Just thinking about my father's broken promise was like a knife to the gut. Getting this wine back was my way to prove to them all that I don't need any man to do my bidding. That I alone am capable of running the business successfully. And most importantly, that I get to decide who I marry. I will not be pawned off to settle a loan.

"And they just let you leave without an answer?" she asked incredulously.

"No, I jumped out my window."

"Of course you did." She chuckled and shook her head. "Okay, since there's a marriage to that fool on the line, I won't try to stop you. But will you at least *try* to be safe traveling at night?" Forever the responsible one in our friendship, and I adored her for that. We balanced each other out. While I jumped out of windows and ran away to chase mutineers in the middle of the night, she'd spend the rest of the night tending to her wounded husband and cross stitching.

She raised a fair point, traveling at night was a double-edged sword. A particularly sharp sword for a woman traveling alone. On one hand, there were a lot fewer people on the roads. On the other, the percentage of those people who posed a threat greatly increased with the setting sun. But I couldn't risk waiting until morning and my parents realizing I was gone before I had time to put distance between me and New Bern.

"You know me, Abby, in the dark with a cloak—I'll be fine." I wasn't a particularly petite woman; my frame was lean and long. When I wrapped my cloak tightly closed so it completely covered my dress, my hood pulled up and hanging low on my face, no one would guess I was a woman. "And you can lend me one of Malcolm's knives if it makes you feel better." And I would feel a bit better too, if I was being honest. After all, I was hunting down mutinous criminals and I would be lying if I said I wasn't at least a bit nervous. But I wasn't going to let a little fear stop me.

Abigail went to go search for a knife and I noticed a bright emerald green cloak hanging on a hook by the door. "Do you still wear this silly thing?" Me and Abby, both without any siblings, used to pretend we were twins. As little girls, we would always try to dress the same and would tell people we were twins. When we were about thirteen years old, my mother made us matching green silk cloaks. It was a sweet gesture, but I wasn't a child anymore and didn't need to play dress up.

"The silk is perfect for summer." She handed me a small hunting knife in a leather sheath attached to a belt. "But won't your parents realize you're gone if Lord Thomas is waiting for an answer?"

"I told them I was feeling faint and needed to go to bed, you know how the lord loves a meek woman. I locked my bedroom door, so if my parents come to check on me, they will think I am ignoring them." At least, I hoped that would be the case. "Speaking of Lord Thomas, do you think I could also take that necklace he gave me that I passed along to you? When I return, I'll give you three more—you should see the last one he gave me" I'd brokered enough deals to know that it never hurt having an extra something to persuade the other person you were worth doing business with.

36

"And tomorrow? You know this is the first place they'll look." She rummaged through a jewelry box. "I won't lie to them, Sloane." Having found the diamond and sapphire necklace, she put it in my hand.

"And you don't have to. Tell them about my late-night visit and while they are figuring out what to do with their runaway—possibly insane—daughter, I'll already be in Beaufort."

"Possibly insane? I would say definitely." She gave me a tight hug before finally letting me leave.

• • •

After a mostly uneventful ride for hours, I thought I was going to make it to Beaufort, a bustling maritime town, without incident. Until I spotted them.

A group of three men, heavily armed with swords and pistols, began to slow their horses as they approached, coming from the other direction. My heart began to pound so loudly I worried they might hear it. My hands started to shake around the reins and Gerty's ears perked up, sensing my anxiety. Encountering highway robbers was an almost certain possibility and I called myself all sorts of obscenities. *Traveling alone at night, with only a dinky, little knife, what was I thinking?!*

When I was a child, I would drive my mother mad by bringing toads, bunnies, and squirrels into the house. Or taking off in the middle of my tutoring lessons to jump in the pond. My father always said my impulsivity would get me in trouble one day. As the three figures on horseback approached me, their long blades bouncing on their horses' haunches, I wondered if that day had come.

To my surprise and amazed relief, the men offered a short greeting and then continued on their way. I was so shaken, I kept looking over my shoulder for the next half hour, expecting to see them charging at me, guns raised, their trouble-free passing just a ruse. But they never came.

I suppose it was my lack of any travel belongings that made them uninterested. With no visible saddle bags, wagon, or cart they must have assumed I had nothing worth stealing. First lucky break. I could only hope I would be as lucky executing the rest of my plan.

I arrived in town just before dawn. Beaufort was a quaint, fishing village that was nestled on the tip of a peninsula facing the Atlantic. They were rich in resources, fishing, whaling, shipbuilding, production of lumber and naval stores. But they struggled with commerce because of their remote location. For this reason, my father and I had visited Beaufort many times; we could market their goods to New Bern and other larger towns.

These trips made Beaufort somewhat of a parallel world for me. It was a place where I was simply a merchant's daughter helping with the family business. There was no talk of eligible bachelors or pressure on my increasing age. I could be exactly who I wanted to be in Beaufort, and I loved the little town for that.

Even though the sun was just barely coloring the sky in a rusty blush, the hardworking people of Beaufort had already started their day. I rode through the small village, taking in the smells—hot bread, fresh cut timber, marshy sea air and fish. Lots and lots of fish. If it wasn't for my nostalgia for the place, I would have found the thick fishy smell nauseating.

I came to stop outside of the weather-battered Dogwood Inn and handed Gerty off to the groom to be fed and watered. I saw two men passed out against the outside wall of the inn. I could hear the sound of drunk men bellowing inside, but the horse hitch was empty, so I figured the mutineers were the guests of honor, having arrived by ship instead of horseback. Walking in, the strong smell of yeast and sweaty bodies mingled with the muggy sea air hit me like a wall.

Inside, the sight was like any other tavern whose festivities had continued to daybreak. Except the men gathered here had an edge to them. I don't know if it was a look in their eyes that said they were looking for a fight. Or if it was the fact that the men with a black eye or a busted lip looked invigorated and strengthened by their recent fights. It could also have been the images of Malcolm's flayed abdomen as he was dragged off the gangway and the knowledge that these men were responsible.

Usually, walking into the tavern that occupied the first floor of the inn brought back positive memories of past trips. The table in the corner was the first time I had tried clam chowder. The large, round table in the center was where my father won big in a game of dice. I could still hear the cheers, the moans of complaints from the losers and the sound of ale mugs being sloshed back and pounded on the table.

"Good lord, if it isn't Sloane Sinclair." Margaret, the innkeeper, came out from behind the bar. Her bird's nest of coarse, grey hair was piled sloppily under a bonnet. Her face wore more lines and sun damage since last I'd seen her, but her green eyes still shone like emeralds in a necklace. Malcolm had started making the Beaufort trips, so it had been five years since I'd seen her.

"Mistress Margaret, your eyes are still sharp as a hawk," I said as she pulled me into a hug and mumbled something under her breath about what a lady I'd become.

"Come, come, sit!" She pushed me toward a stool at the bar. "I suppose ye'll be hungry, no?"

"I would give my right hand for some bacon and your famous corn dodgers right now." I had been so focused on reaching Beaufort, I hadn't realized how absolutely ravenous I was.

"Of course, of course, my dear. And yer father will be wantin' some too?"

"He didn't come with me on this trip, but I'm happy to eat his portion," I joked.

"Is he well?" I knew Margaret held my father in a special place in her heart. After a hurricane took off the roof of the inn and flooded the tavern, he gave her a loan to repair the damage. A loan he coincidentally never asked to be paid back.

"He is," I said. "Just preoccupied at the moment." She returned my smile before bustling into the kitchen.

It was unsettling sitting at the bar with my back to the drunk men. A chill ran up my spine and I turned around. It was like sneaking into a den of wolves as a rabbit they hadn't spotted yet. Currently, the wolves were singing a Gaelic song, pounding a beat on the tables. At the end of the song, they swayed to their feet and attempted to cheers one another. Half of them missed their companions' mug and ale spilled over the floor and table. They didn't look nearly as intimidating when they could barely stand on their own.

If they were that long into the drink, I knew they weren't planning on leaving anytime soon. I poked my head into the kitchen and hollered at Margaret, "I'm going to find myself a spare bed upstairs, I'll be down later for the dodgers!" As hungry as I was, I couldn't stand being in the men's presence for a second longer.

• • •

"Now will ye tell me what ye're doing here all alone?" Margret settled on the edge of the bed next to me, setting a platter of food on the dresser.

"Those soldiers downstairs aren't what they seem." She urged me to continue with a silent nod. "There was a mutiny, and they killed their captain and anyone who didn't support them" I told her everything about the wine, the raid, the aftermath. She didn't seem all that surprised by the events—granted, she had her own horror stories at sea.

She immigrated to the colonies with her husband and four teenage daughters. But shortly after they set sail, there was a pox outbreak. She'd had the pox as a child so avoided getting it again, but husband and daughters didn't have the same protection. Without proper medical care on board and the already filthy conditions, the disease ravaged the ship.

Margaret left England with her family, hopeful and excited about all the adventures and opportunities they'd have in the New World. But by the time she arrived in North

Carolina, she was all alone, all her children and husband returned to the sea.

"And what exactly are ye plannin' on doing, lass?"

"I'm going to go to the garrison, tell the colonel what's happened, and get our wine back." She looked concerned for the first time in our entire conversation.

"Do ye think that's wise? Ye're like a daughter to me, Sloane; I dinna want ye gettin' yerself hurt. These soldier-types tend to stick together, who's to say the colonel isn't in on it too?"

"I have to put this right, Margaret. The colonel knows my father, he went through us for a lot of the garrison's supplies. He's an honest man."

"I don't suppose there's any talking ye out of this? These are dangerous men."

"I didn't travel all through the night to get cold feet now. But there's no danger at present, they don't know who I am or why I'm here. You're the only person who knows, and I know you won't tell anyone."

"I would never." She patted my knee. The hallway creaked outside the room. I looked up panicked, *was someone listening through the door*? "Don't worry, love, this house creaks every time a mouse breathes. If someone was in the hallway, we'd have heard the steps."

"There is one thing you could help me with." I looked down at my dress, splattered with mud at the hem and stiff with sweat from my long ride.

"Anything, dear." Her warm smile and willingness to always lend a hand lightened my spirits. For all the terrible evil in the world, there was still more good in the world because of people like Margaret.

"I only have one chance to make my case to the colonel and I don't think this dress will do me any favors...do you have anything I could borrow?"

"I know just the thing." She raised her eyebrows at me the way mothers do right before they give you an order. "But ye look exhausted, rest now and when ye're ready, come down and I'll get ye sorted."

"You're the best." I gave her another hug before she stood up and left the room.

The bed was not very comfortable, nor very clean, but as soon as I was horizontal, I didn't care. It had indeed been a long day and a longer night; I was asleep quicker than the mutineers were throwing back shots of whiskey.

CHAPTER FIVE

Striking First

"Mind yer head at the top." I followed behind Margaret up to the attic, ducking on the last rung.

For an attic, it was surprisingly tidy. Food stuffs were neatly organized on one side and three large trunks lined the other side. There were no cobwebs in the corners that were practically customary in all attics, and the air actually smelled a bit like lavender.

"This is the nicest attic I've ever seen." I found the source of the lavender, a dried bunch of the flowers hung from the drafters.

"Oh, it's silly really, but it's my favorite place in the inn. Always quiet and free of any drunk fools." She looked at the floorboards where below, the lodgers were eating the evening meal and socializing loudly. "So, whenever I need a wee break, I come up. Here, let me show ye."

The back wall was lined with shelves stocked with canned goods. She pushed on it, and I was stunned when the middle portion of the shelves rotated on a center axis. Behind the trick door was a small room, which turned ambient orange when Margaret lit a candle.

There was a rocking chair in one corner with heavy knit blankets draped over the back. A small side table with the lit candle and a stack of books. It was quite a lovely reading nook, but what was it doing in a secret room in the Dogwood Inn's attic?

"Margaret, what is this place?"

"I first came up with the idea, when I wanted a secure place to keep my few precious belongings. With so many people comin' and goin' all the time, I thought it wise. But when I started coming up here for a little peace and quiet, I decided to make it a bit more comfortable for myself."

I could relate to the need to have some space of your own, some breathing room from the hectic demands of daily life. My moonlit rides with Gerty were that for me.

"This is why I brought ye here." Margaret had knelt down beside a trunk and was holding up a beautiful dress she'd pulled out of it. "It was my eldest daughter's. I couldna bear to get rid of it."

"Margaret, it's gorgeous." The dress was pale olive green printed with a delicate and sophisticated floral pattern of gold and muted blue. Thick, gold embroidery traced the hem of the dress and sleeve ruffles were lined with white lace.

"The colonel won't be able to say no to ye in this." She winked and pulled out the rest of the petticoats, stay, and stomacher.

Margaret helped me get dressed in my room and even helped plait my hair, weaving a matching blue ribbon through it. My heart rate was already increasing with nerves, but once she laced up the back of my stay, it became ever more difficult to breathe. Damn the women who decided that struggling to breathe was fashionable. She yanked on the strings, tying it so tight my breasts were nearly spilling out.

"I've found there's often a correlation between how tight a woman's stay is and how persuasive men find her." Margaret patted my back and continued working on my hair. I hated to admit that she did have a point. But my thoughts were elsewhere. The inevitable deluge of what-if's spiraled in my head.

What if it's a new colonel and he is just as corrupt as the sailors?

What if he doesn't believe me and I'm arrested for making a false claim?

What if the ship has already left and the wine's gone forever?

At least, I never questioned my own resolve. If I chickened out and didn't go to the garrison, my family would face losing the business and the warehouse or settling for a marriage to Lord Thomas. Following through with the plan at least gave me a chance to put things right.

Of course, all those things could still happen if my plan didn't work... *Shut up, Sloane*—I forced myself to push that dreary thought out of my mind.

"Now give it a twirl, lass." Margaret finished pinning up my braided hair. and stepped back to appreciate her handiwork. I obliged her with a slow spin to show off the dress from all angles. "Seeing ye in that dress, seeing it enjoyed again—" She wiped a tear. "It does something for a grievin' heart."

I wrapped her in my arms, touched by her words. Apparently, this was a big day for the both of us.

• • •

When I left the Dogwood, there were only a few men I recognized from the morning quietly playing dice in the corner. *Where were the rest of the crew?* Probably sleeping off their hangovers. Well, good. I didn't need a whole pack of them seeing me leave and wondering where I was going.

One of the men playing dice followed me across the tavern floor with his eyes. I felt them burning my back as I watched him in my peripheral vision. At the door, I looked back, and our eyes met over his ale mug as he drank.

There was a certain intensity to his stare that made the hairs on my arm stand up and a chill at the back of my neck. I don't know what it was about him that was so unsettling.

Maybe it was the way he didn't avert his gaze when I caught him staring. But really, I think it was more the surety with which he stared back, as if he knew me and was waiting for me to recognize him. Whatever it was wasn't going to get me any closer to getting my wine back. I shook off the unease and walked out the door, chalking the experience up to showtime anxiety.

The air in the streets was heavy and the clouds were darkening. The dress sat just off my shoulders, and I felt small rain drops on my bared skin. Good thing I wasn't one to believe in omens, because I don't think it starting to rain would be a good sign.

I took the route along the harbor, the garrison being at the end of it. The dusk kept peeking in and out of the drizzle. The fishermen were hauling in their nets for the evening, probably in a hurry to get home for dinner.

I heard a distressing noise come from an alley that ran into the harbor. It sounded like a wailing child.

Sure enough, when I turned down the alley, there was a young babe wrapped in cloth lying on the muddy ground. *What in the world?*

Something was off, I could feel it. But I also couldn't leave a crying baby in the muddy street without at least checking to see if it was okay.

As I neared the infant I could see there was a note pinned to its swaddle. This made me drop my guard a little. I'd heard of unfit mothers dropping their child off at a church or on a neighbor's porch with a note surrendering their rights. But I'd never heard of a babe being left in a harbor alley...

I jumped back in surprise. When I was just a few feet away from the babe, a woman popped out from behind a stack of wooden boxes. She swooped in and snatched up the child who instantly stopped crying in her arms. *The mother?*

"I'm sorry, lord forgive me," she said to me with a pained look on her face before running away.

Instantly, a vice-like grip yanked my arms behind my back and I felt the cool metal of a blade at my throat.

It was a trap.

"I'd strongly advise against screaming, love." The voice was low and raw, seethed with matter-of-fact hatred. I could hear it in his voice, he would slit my throat without blinking. I swallowed slowly, feeling the blade cut deeper as I did.

A rough fabric was tied around my head, blindfolding me.

I always thought I would be the type of person who fought back if attacked. My father had taught me how to punch and I liked to think of myself as fearless. But as men I couldn't see gagged me and bound my hands with frightening efficiency, it was all I could do to keep my knees from giving out. I didn't have to worry about that for much longer though because someone lifted me from the ground and threw me upside down across their shoulder.

"Do ye feel this?" the harsh voice spoke again as a hard, small surface pressed against my temple, "That's a pistol and it would take a miracle to miss at this distance." He laughed and my stomach took a sickening drop. "So, don't try anything stupid, eh?" I nodded, feeling the barrel move along with my head.

I didn't need to ask who they were or what they wanted. The trap was set so I would walk by it at just the right time. They didn't demand money or jewelry; they simply took me. I thought back to the man I saw while leaving the inn. The mutineers had figured out—or were told—my intentions and were striking first.

Looks like today was the day my impulsivity would get me in trouble after all.

I heard the footsteps around me change to that hollow sound of walking on wood, we were boarding their ship.

Panic rippled through me as I realized that if I boarded this ship, there was a good chance I wouldn't be leaving it alive. Like a jolt of lightning, I returned from the frightened space in my head to my body.

I arched my back and tried to fling myself off my captor's shoulder. This only resulted in me squirming like an ornery child in his arms. Frustrated, I swung my legs wildly, trying to hit any part of him I could.

I must have gotten lucky because he groaned loudly before dropping me unceremoniously on my back. My wrists seared with pain as they caught my fall, my hands still bound behind my back.

In the commotion, my blindfold had shifted and for the first time, I caught a glimpse of my attackers. Three men towered over me, peering down, their brutish faces running the gamut between amused and irate. Behind them, I spotted another man hunched over, clutching his crotch. Despite the tension, I couldn't help but feel a bit pleased that I had succeeded in doing a little damage.

"I'm gettin' real tired of ye already," the ugliest of the bunch growled. I recognized his voice as the man who held the knife to my throat. He shoved his fingers down the front of my dress and aggressively pulled me to my feet by my stay. His hand jumped from my dress to my throat, and I let out an involuntary gasp. Was this how I was going to die? At least I'd go out knowing I fought back.

Just as I was expecting him to tighten his grip, he let go and turned away. I choked on air and fought back tears.

In a blur of movement, he spun around to deliver a massive blow to my jaw. I barely had a second to register the splitting pain before everything went black.

• • •

I awoke to the gentle lull of being on the water. For those brief seconds after I woke but before I opened my eyes, I wondered how I'd gotten on a ship. The putrid smell of the hull and the metal biting at my ankles brought me back to reality.

The night before, when I came to after losing consciousness, I discovered I was chained by the ankles and wrists to a bolt drilled into the hull of the mutineer's ship. I spent hours fruitlessly tugging on the chains and cursing Margaret for what she did. I spent so long tugging that my ankles started bleeding through my stockings from the friction. The manacles were jagged with rust and quickly turned my wrists equally raw.

But none of it hurt nearly as much as being stabbed in the back by Margaret. In fact, literally being stabbed in the back would hurt less.

I was so touched by her words when she saw me in her daughter's dress, but I guess it was all crocodile tears. Was it even her daughter's dress or was that just another lie? She made me a sacrificial lamb and for what deity? Evil, mutinous men? It didn't make any sense. But she was the only one in the entire town that knew my plans. It could have only been her who alerted them.

I tested moving my jaw and found it wasn't as sore as the night before. Well, that was one positive in this unbelievable disaster I had found myself.

My stomach panged with hunger and I figured it was time enough my *hosts* showed a bit of hospitality.

"I'm hungry, you bloody bastards!" They may be tired of me, but I can guarantee I was even more sick of them.

Almost immediately, I heard the sound of a key turning and the lock clicked behind the door. A string bean of a young man stepped out from behind the door as if he was walking into a lion's cage.

"Mistress?" His brown eyes looked down at my bloody wrists, eyes widened and then quickly averted his gaze. *Was he uncomfortable keeping me chained like an animal?* He might be another crew member like the one Malcolm met. Unsettled by the mutiny but caught in the current out of fear.

"Get me your captain, please. And something to eat."

• • •

A man built like an ox busted through the door with such force it banged loudly against the back wall, making me jump. His shaved head was veiny and marred with scars and his face looked like it had been stuck in a scowl for years. I balled my fists to keep my hands from trembling. Just having his glare narrowed in on me was more terrifying than having a knife to my throat. For the hundredth time since I'd left Abigail's house, I wondered what the hell I was thinking.

"So, ye're the wee bitch who tried to ruin everything, huh?" His voice was hoarse. Refusing to let his frightening presence distract me from my plan, I rose to my feet.

"You have something I want, and I have something you need."

His eyes roamed my body, resting on my breasts. "I bet ye do, lass."

"The wine. I want it." His eyes narrowed. Before I left Margaret's, I had sown the diamond necklace I took from Abigail into the lining of my petticoat. I reached under the open front of my gown and into the pocket slit of my petticoat and tore the necklace from its stitching.

"I have much more." I threw the necklace at his feet. "Enough to buy the whole shipment three times over." *Okay, that was a bit of an exaggeration, but he didn't know that.*

"What are ye proposing, lass?"

"A trade. You have a ship full of imported, *stolen,* French wine and brandy." He flinched at the words stolen. *Good,* I thought, I wanted him on edge, to feel the pressure mounting. That was one of the first lessons in selling my father taught me—people never buy later, they only buy now; and they won't buy now unless there's urgency making them buy *now.* I figured hostage negotiations were close enough to sales. I hoped I was right.

"You have two options—One, make your way to the Bahamas and hope that you can fence the wine for a fraction of what it's worth without the Crown's certificate. That's if you can make it through the pirate routes in an English military ship without being attacked. Or two, give me the entire shipment in a more than fair exchange for jewelry that will sell much easier and for much more."

He withdrew a pistol from his side. "And what's to stop me from shootin' ye right now and taking the wine and the necklace?" He was trying to intimidate me, but I knew I was still in control of this deal despite being the one chained. I was right and he knew it. He would have a very hard time turning a profit with the wine, and even if I was bluffing and the jewelry in front of me was all I had, it would still be a life changing amount to a man like him.

"Nothing," I said. "Except losing the chance to become a very rich man."

He made a noncommittal grunt, and his permanent scowl held a touch of puzzlement. I unclenched my fists, satisfied they were no longer shaking. As he paced in front of me, I got a foul whiff of his body odor. I had defused the immediate threat to my safety and actually felt pretty good about establishing the trade. *Hopeful optimism?* Maybe, but I didn't have many other options.

Without another word to me, he left the hold. "Get the whore something to eat," he said to the string bean.

• • •

The young man returned with a tray of food but didn't move from the door. The ox filed in after him, trailed by another man.

"Forgive me manners, I forgot to introduce myself. Ye can call me Captain Baker and I'm known to be a greedy man, my lady." His hungry grin made my stomach churn. "And ye see, I think we can get a lot more out of you than a few pebbles." He pushed forward an older looking man with spectacles that sat low on his nose. He dropped sheets of parchment and a quill at my feet.

"Yer gonna write us a pretty little letter, eh? Let your parents know they won't be getting you or the wine back for anything less than five thousand pieces of eight." *Like hell I would drag my parents deeper into this.* They wouldn't lose any more money because of me. Then I noticed something was missing and smiled.

"What do you want me to say?" I asked.

"Tell them to bring the five thousand to Charleston in a week's time if they ever want to see ye alive again."

I obliged and started scratching the quill across the paper.

"Ye useless idiot," Baker bellowed to the older man when he realized my writing was leaving no words. "Ye forgot the bloody ink!" Looking like he was about to lose his head, the man ran scared out the door, returning less than a minute later with an ink bottle

"Sir." He handed it to Baker, his head bowed. I could tell his hand was shaking by the ink wavering in the bottle.

"Write." He gave me the ink, scowling. I finished the letter and handed it to him. He then gave it to the other man. "Read it." The man cleared his throat and began

"*Dear Father and Mother, I have been taken by smelly ugly pigs. Please come save me from this horrid sty.*"

"Stupid bitch."

His heavy booted foot plowed into my stomach. His kick knocked all the wind out of me, and I crumbled like the piece of paper he was now crunching in his fist. "Write it again," he growled.

Still feeling breathless, I wrote another letter and handed it to the literate man.

"*Dear Father and Mother, I was taken by mutineers who demand a ransom of five thousand pieces of eight.*"

The captain grinned satisfied. *"However, they have all turned into mermaids so you can ignore their request. Sincerely—"*

Another forceful kick to my gut cut him off.

Another letter written and read. *"Dear Mother and Father, I was taken by a crew of mutineers. Do not fear for me, they have welcomed me as their new leader. It's a pirate's life for me!"*

I coughed and gagged from the next kick but tolerated the pain for the rush of satisfaction I got each time Baker's face scrunched up in anger. I may be chained, beaten, and with no prospects of escape, but being able to get under his skin like this made me feel like I had regained a little power.

In his assault on me, he had kicked over the ink bottle, black liquid spilling across the floor. He shouted a slew of obscenities and stormed out of the room like a giant toddler throwing a tantrum.

Once he left, the string bean hesitantly set down the plate of food. A heel of moldy bread, dry and crumbly, and a mug of ale to wash it down. I didn't have the energy to complain nor mind and picked the moldy bits off. He immediately returned to his station at the door, gaze set on the back of the hold above my head, never meeting my eyes.

He seemed scared, that much was for sure. He tapped his right boot in subtle but anxious beats. He kept double checking his musket loading, running the ramrod every few minutes. Every time there were footsteps or shuffling behind the door, his head would spin around, and his grip would tighten to white knuckles on his weapon.

Picking up my mug, I bumped the chain connecting my two wrists. The movement dragged the rough metal over my raw skin, and I winced audibly. For the first time, he looked me in the eyes, his knitted together in a painfully apologetic frown. He looked away immediately, seemingly disturbed that he let his mask fall. But I already saw it.

"What's your name, sir?" He clearly did not like this situation and perhaps I could use his empathy to my advantage. He looked around as if seeking permission to speak to me.

"Fraser, ma'am. Charlie Fraser." He had a Scottish accent and my heart panged with longing for my father. To think of the fear and anger he must be feeling right now. His only daughter, stolen because she acted like a damn, trusting fool. He would know what to do right now, were he in my situation. What would he do? Build trust and forge a connection, the foundation to any deal.

"Fraser as in Clan Fraser? My father grew up on Fraser land, speaks fondly of the Fraser men." He nodded, didn't say a word, but did meet my eyes. *Progress.* "So, tell me, Charlie, how'd you end up with this crew?"

"Stealin'." He stared down at his boots. "My Da was too deep in the drink to provide for the family, so my wee brother took to swiping food while I was off working on the road. I came home to him in the stocks," he cleared his throat. "I know I shouldna left. Shoulda stayed with my family there, kept watch of the bairns when Da failed." I could feel the guilt and shame in his voice, I don't know how long ago this was, but he clearly still felt responsible for his brother's misadventures.

57

"You were simply trying to provide. I bet you planned on giving all your coin to your family upon return, no?" I had to make him feel safe and not judged. His story was not an uncommon one, but that doesn't make it any less painful for those involved. My father's hard work left us never wanting, but I knew I was one of the lucky few who never had to worry where their next meal was coming from.

"Sure did. But instead, the redcoats came through pressing convicted men into service. My brother was too young, so they took me in his place."

"Can they do that? You did nothing wrong."

"That doesna matter to them."

"And the mutiny? You didn't want to be a part of it, did you?"

"No, Mistress. I am ashamed to be part of it. It pains me to see you chained so." This was my opening. I did feel sorry for him, he had not had it easy, and misfortune seemed to follow him like the plague. But I saw an opportunity and had to take it.

"My wrists hurt something fierce, it's hard to eat with them like this." I exaggerated a grimace as I tore off a bite of bread and the metal grated against my bloodied skin.

"Let me." The chance to be chivalrous seemed to light up his eyes and he took several steps toward me, pulling out a key.

"Oh no, I would never forgive myself if you got in trouble for your kindness." *But please, get these damned things off me!*

"Just the wrists, eh? While you eat. It's not like ye'll be going anywhere with 'em still shackled to yer ankles." His tone was faster and more excited than the sullen monotone he previously spoke in. I guessed some small bit of the weight on his shoulders chipped away by helping me. He was a good man caught up in a monster's den.

The chains clattered to the floor, and I grabbed his hand as he stood up. "Thank you, Charlie, sincerely." His mouth turned up in a subtle smile.

CHAPTER SIX

Visitors

The entirety of the ship shook seconds after hearing the roar of a cannon and the exploding sound of splintering wood followed the crew's screams. I froze, stunned, and Charlie darted out of the hold, snatching up his rifle by the door.

Another cannon blast shook the ship. I could hardly believe my change in luck. Tears of gratitude and relief pricked my eyes: The authorities must have learned about Baker and his mutiny. And now the military had chased down the ship and had come to take it back. I knew the mutineers didn't stand a chance against a planned and fully manned attack from English troops.

It sounded like absolute chaos. I could smell the sulfur gunpowder all the way below deck and the sounds of gunfire came in rapid succession. The clash of metal and high-pitch screams mingled with bass howls and indecipherable shouts. Every now and then something would land on the deck above with a loud thump making me jump. A body hitting the deck.

"Help!" I shouted, trying to be heard over the angry sounds of fighting above me. "I'm down here! Help!" While the fight continued to rage, my cries for help were fruitless.

Only a few minutes after the first cannon blast, the commotion above stopped. As suddenly as the battle began, it appeared to stop. All I could hear were muffled voices and the scuffling of feet. There was a hazy quality to the air from all the fired ammunition that I could taste on my tongue—chalky, bitter and smokey.

"Help, down here!" I started shouting again. I pulled desperately on my ankle chains screwed into floorboards. I couldn't stand to be stuck down here for a minute longer. This nightmare was finally coming to an end, help was here and I didn't want to wait...or risk being left behind! *What would happen if they never found me down here?* My excitement turned to panic, and I tugged as if my life depended on it, as it very well might.

At last, the door swung open.

Standing in the doorway was a man with his clothes in near rags, his long, dark hair loose like a mane and crimson blood splattered his face and chest. A pistol was tucked into his belt and his sword dangled from his hand, still dripping with blood.

*He's not an agent of the Crown...*my mind raced to make sense of the scene in front of me, until finally it came to a horrifying conclusion. The ship had not been stormed by English soldiers on a rescue mission. It had been raided by pirates.

Whatever horrible mental images I'd had of pirates before, the reality was much worse. As I watched blood slide down the tip of his blade, splattering the floor in red, I realized that the nightmare that had begun when I was kidnapped was far from over. My stomach churned, my face broke out in a cold sweat and I became sick all over the floorboards.

"Yeesh, am I that ugly, eh?" The pirate chuckled at his own joke.

I glimpsed my wrist chains limp on the floor. My only possible means of self-defense. Though, who was I kidding, this man was literally dripping in blood, I doubted I'd be able to even scratch him. But I couldn't do nothing either— what would my father say if I didn't even try to fight back?

I threw myself to my knees as if I was going to retch again. My skirt billowed out and covered the chains.

"A regular prince charming," I muttered under my breath.

"Captain! We got a prize ye're gonna want to see down here," he shouted over his shoulder. He sauntered toward me, head cocked to one side, eyes hungrily taking in my defenseless position chained to the floor.

"Captain won't mind me inspecting the goods first, eh?" he said with a lascivious grin. He stepped forward and I pulled the chain out from under my skirt and leaped to my feet.

I swung the chain at his head. He easily ducked and laughed at my attempt. "Verra good try, lass."

He pulled the pistol from his belt and aimed it directly at my head. "Now, drop that wee chain or I'll blow your head off," He shrugged, "It really doesn't make a difference to me which."

My eyes locked on the barrel of the pistol, I tossed the chain in front of me. He kicked it away. I felt like crying watching my one line of defense slide across the floor out of reach.

I took a step back for every step he took forward, until the length of my chain ran out and I stumbled backward. My head met the hard wood with a thunk, and I heard the pirate laugh at my clumsiness. I tried to sit up, but the weight of his body was quickly on top of me, flattening me to the floor.

I screamed for help—not knowing what good it would do me on a ship full of pirates just as blood thirsty from the raid as my attacker.

His groping hands tried to push up my layers of skirt and petticoat while I kicked and flailed my legs desperately. Terrified as the brute got closer and closer to his goal despite my best attempts to kick him off, I burst into hot tears. I could taste the salty tears as they slid down to my mouth and my vision blurred with moisture.

I couldn't believe how far down into the darkness my situation had spiraled. Kidnapped, beaten, chained, and now I was going to be raped by a pirate.

Suddenly, his weight was no longer on me. In shock, I lay paralyzed on the floor until the excruciating sound of bone on bone snapped me back to the present.

I pushed myself up just in time to see my attacker clutching his bleeding, and presumably broken, nose.

Standing in front of him was an imposing broad-chested figure with long, wild hair and black soot smeared in a long wide stroke from his right temple to left jawbone.

His shirt was stained with so much blood that I could smell the metallic. I would bet my last dollar that none of that blood was his. I'd heard the stories of brutal pirates, regular seamen turned into murderers and plunderers. But this was no ordinary man. He was the monster that inhabits people's worst nightmares.

"Get outta my sight." His growl sent my attacker scuttling from the room. The man who attacked me was the scariest man I'd ever encountered. My body was still shaking with fear from the assault. And yet, this new blood-drenched pirate sent him running away with his tail between his legs.

He outstretched his open palm. "Take my hand, lass."

His hand was smeared with blood, and I stared at it, unbelievably terrified. He wiped his palm on his pants and then offered his hand again. When his hand remained empty, he shrugged it away. "Suit yerself."

He kneeled down and his eyes, the color of the sea caught in a storm, met mine. For some reason, the fact that rabbits' hearts can stop from fear alone popped into my head—literally being scared to death. Was this the captain that my attacker had first called? Was he here to finish the job? Bile rose in my throat, and I squeezed my eyes shut waiting for the worst. If he didn't kill me himself, I would probably die of fright.

But instead of stopping my heart, he pulled out a ring of keys from his waistband and began trying keys in the lock that secured my ankles. Once he found a fit and the chains were removed, he grabbed my hand and pulled me to my feet.

He ran his fingertips across the inside of my wrist where the skin was still pink and chaffed. I was surprised by the tenderness of his touch. The light friction burned slightly but he remained gentle. But his gentle touch did nothing to erase the blood stains and violence I knew he'd just committed. "Are yer ankles bad too?"

"Worse." I yanked my hand out of his and shot him a glare. *I didn't take your hand the first time for a reason.*

"Follow me."

"I am not following you anywhere." I crossed my arms like a defiant child. He sighed, wrapped his arm around my waist, and tried to move me forward as I dug my heels in.

"Get your filthy hands off me!" I shook out of his grasp.

"Given the fact that ye were chained to the floor and dressed like a whore—" His eyes scanned the length of my body, coming to rest on my absurdly pushed-up breasts. My cheeks instantly burned red. "I highly doubt ye're a willing passenger. Now, ye can either stay here with a half-dead crew or ye can count yer lucky stars and follow me."

Was there even a choice? I was somewhere in the middle of the ocean and my only chance of getting anywhere near land was if a crew with beating hearts was manning the ship.

"Fine." *But I'm not happy about it.* I shot him a look, daring him to put his hands on me one more time. "But I can walk just fine on my own."

As I left the hold, I saw Charlie. He lay sprawled out, his abdomen soaked in blood, his musket next to him, just out of reach. The one man who showed me kindness, who just wanted to do right by his family, dead. He didn't stand a chance against monsters like the pirates. The sight immediately called to mind the look of anguish and loss in my father's eyes when he told me about his brother's death. I pictured the young boy, losing blood and life from the wood lodged in his neck, and shivered with a wave of nausea.

"If ye can walk so well on yer own, how 'bout ye actually do it, aye?" the pirate said.

I hadn't even realized I had stopped moving. I tried to take another step forward, but a wave of nausea washed over me.

"Or do I have to throw ye over my shoulder and carry ye off this damn ship?"

"You wouldn't dare." I shot him my most threatening glare that almost certainly was like being stared at by a fresh kitten to him.

"Then keep movin'."

The top deck of the ship was what I imagined a battlefield would look like. Men were strewn across the deck in various stages of injury. Some merely battered and bruised but sitting up on their own, hands bound while a pirate armed with a rifle kept an eye on them. Some lay in growing pools of ruby, the only sign of life their stomach slowly rising and falling. Others lay lifeless with still bellies and gruesome, slashed throats.

As I followed my pirate guide, men transporting goods from one ship to the other stopped and stared. I felt like a wounded deer being circled by hungry wolves. I took all of their ravenous looks as direct threats. Feeling incredibly overwhelmed all at once, my legs shaky, I grabbed onto my guide's arm for support.

His hard bicep under my hand felt like an anchor and I hated that I was comforted when he placed his hand on top of mine and whispered, "It's alright, lass, we're almost there."

We crossed a gangplank onto the pirate ship, the ocean swirled beneath my feet, and I felt like I was crossing the River Styx into Hades. He led me all the way back to the highest deck on the stern where there was no one else.

I leaned against the taffrail, gulping in the fresh air, begging my heart to slow its panicked racing. I wanted to scream into the wind. Pushing back tears and taking a moment to compose myself again, I spun around to face the pirate. "Who are you?"

"Captain Elliot Cross at yer service, my lady." He gave me a small bow. I couldn't tell if he was mocking me or being genuine given that just moments ago, he was threatening to throw me over his shoulder. Which I didn't doubt he was capable of. Every part of him seemed to be chiseled out of a block of marble.

The contours of his sculpted chest created sharp ridges underneath his tattered and bloodied shirt and his broad, square shoulders created an arresting figure of strength. Layered with sweat, blood, and soot, his pronounced bone structure reminded me of a gargoyle. The black soot contrasted with his eyes, making them shine a cold, icy blue like snow in the moonlight. His whole body was taut with lean muscle, a finely-honed weapon.

"So, what now?"

"Come." He led me below deck to a small wooden cell located deep in the back of the ship's storage hold. He motioned me to enter the cell.

"No." I said.

"No, what?"

"No, I am not going in that decrepit cage." I made a move to walk away, but he gripped me by the shoulders, stopping me.

"I promise this is to keep them out." With a nod, he indicated to the rest of the crew above deck. "Not to keep ye in." This was clearly a cell for prisoners or punished crew members. Yet, it was supposed to be my safe refuge?

"So, you've taken me from prisoner on one ship to prisoner on another and I'm supposed to—how did you put it—'count my lucky stars?'" I instantly started missing the fresh air above deck and regretted following him like a stupid sheep to this dank armpit of the ship.

"This is only temporary," he reiterated as he spun me around and pushed me inside. He turned the key, and I could hear the heavy lock click into place like a punch to the gut.

"Bastard," I whispered under my breath, just loud enough for him to hear. It was odd, his stormy eyes and mouth drawn in a tight line made him look genuinely regretful. For a moment, I thought he was going to unlock the door. But that apologetic look did not match his deep gravelly voice and blood-soaked clothes that showed who he really was.

"I'll send Jonas down to keep watch," he said before walking away. The hefty metal lock untouched.

To keep watch for me or on me?

I slumped against the wall, defeated. *How did I end up here?* Mere days ago, I was imagining my life at the head of the family business, having successfully broken into the wine trade, my father would be overflowing with pride and wondering how he could have ever doubted me. Lord Thomas would be a distant memory rather than a marriage prospect. And now I was locked in a cage in the bottom of a pirate ship.

I let a few tears slide down my cheek before shaking it off and starting to pace the short distance of my cell. *Enough moping around,* it was time to figure out how the hell to get myself out of yet another impossible situation. First, I would need to confirm that the pirates even had the wine on board. This hunt for this wine got me in this situation and I'd be damned if I left it behind.

My scheming was interrupted by a giant's arrival. His hulking form made him mere inches away from grazing his head on the deck above. This must be Jonas, my guard dog, or more accurately, guard elephant.

He gave a curt nod with a "ma'am," then turned around and stood in position without another word. His boyish face and curly blond hair made his large frame less intimidating. He reminded me of my childhood friend Fergus.

Fergus and I learned to ride horses together. We would spend hot, summer days racing each other until we couldn't bear the heat anymore and jump into the lake. His wet curls would drip down his face and he would shake like a wet dog, water splattering me. I would splash him back until we ended up in a full-blown water fight.

We had so much fun together until one day my mother saw me return home sopping wet. She yelled at me for my indecent behavior, swimming in my undergarments with a boy and forbade Fergus from coming over again. At the time, I was just a young girl and didn't even understand what she was so mad about. All I knew was I couldn't see my good friend anymore.

Remembering my old friend, I called out to Jonas. "Hey, you." He turned to face me. "Do you know what was taken from the other ship?"

"Many things, ma'am." *Not helpful, Jonas.*

"Yes, of course, but what sort of things? Did you notice any wine?"

"Can't say I did, ma'am." *Come on, Jonas, help me out here!*

"Okay, but is there a chance there was wine taken?"

"I suppose there's a chance."

"Jonas!" He looked taken aback by my outburst, but this man of few words was testing my patience. "I don't mean to yell, but it's very important that I find out if there was any wine taken from that ship. Can you help me?"

"Of course, my lady." *A helpful answer at last.* We both looked up at the sounds of footsteps. A boy of no more than ten timidly approached, his eyes glued to his shuffling bare feet. He barely looked up in acknowledgment of his presence when he passed Jonas, and then came to stop in front of my cell.

"Some supper, my lady." He slid a wooden bowl of food in through a slit in the bars. He reminded me of a stray kitten I found behind our stable. His hair was shaggy and dirty, like the kitten's without its mother's grooming. His face was coated in a layer of dirt and grime with a speckling of freckles. I remembered how that little barn kitten, despite being small and weak, hissed and spat at me when I tried to pick it up.

My father asked what happened when he saw my arms cut up like I'd been crawling through blackberry bushes. I lifted the lid of my basket and showed him the orange tabby who'd finally fallen asleep on a pile of napkins.

"He's just now settled down. He put up quite a fight for something so tiny," I had said.

"That's a natural survival instinct. It didn't matter that ye were much bigger than him, he was driven by a burning need to survive. He was all alone, and he had only himself to rely on. He's a braw little one." My father looked down and smiled at the sleeping ball of orange fuzz.

When the young boy finally dared himself to look up at me, I saw in his eyes the same fierce fire of survival. I had no doubt that being a galley boy on a pirate ship wasn't a young boy's first choice in a pastime and a difficult one at that.

From my father's time as a galley boy, I knew life on a ship was often a dog-eat-dog world, especially for the youngest crew members. Even though he was constantly surrounded by others, he said it often felt like he was all alone after his brother died.

He slid the wooden tray between the bars. "The captain wishes to speak with you shortly." He gave me a meek smile and bow, and then walked away.

The food itself didn't look very appealing, a brown sludge with chunks of mystery meat. But the smell was enough to make my mouth water, rich and homely like any proper stew should smell. There was a slice of dry bread on the side. My stomach was cramped with hunger, and I met its growl by shoveling the food into my mouth quicker than my chewing could keep up.

"I don't think I've ever seen someone so eager to devour Cook's food," a deep voice interrupted my feast.

I looked up to find the captain and nearly choked on my food. I stood slowly, brushing the crumbs off my mouth and skirt. I was embarrassed to be caught eating like a dog, but when I remembered that he was a murdering pirate, I suddenly cared much less. *Who is he to judge me?*

He entered the cell, bringing with him a sack of flour and a bundle of thick fabric.

"It's not much, but it's softer than wood," he said as he laid fabric on the floor of the hold. I recognized it as a cloth used to make sails. We sold the same material for a weaver in Wilmington, it sold like hot cakes after hurricane season. Was this supposed to be my bedding?

He unwrapped the sail and revealed a small glass jar and torn strips of linen. "Jonas, please bring me and the lady two crates to sit."

Jonas returned with two wooden crates filled with a grid of dividers and set them before me and Captain Cross. "Sit." He gestured to my crate, and I almost did. But then I saw *Château Pape Clément* written in sweeping letters across the side.

Château Pape Clément was the winery we bought a life saving's worth of wine from.

"Where's the rest of the wine? Have you imbeciles already drunk it all?" I kicked the empty crate that should have been filled with *my* wine.

Jonas popped his head into the cell. "We do have the wine onboard, ma'am." *Obviously.*

"I can see that, Jonas," I snapped. I turned my attention back to the captain. "That's my wine, Captain..." and the rest just poured out of me. The day the ship returned, and men came back bloody and wounded. My trip to Beaufort, and Margaret's betrayal. How Baker kidnapped me and stole my jewelry.

"What's yer name, lass?"

I was shocked again by the contradiction between his coarse, rumbly voice and the softness in his eyes. I expected every part of a pirate captain to be hard and cold. Yet his eyes, pale blue with deep charcoal wisps like storm clouds in the sky, made me feel safe like in the eye of a hurricane. *Safe? How can you feel safe around a pirate?* I scolded myself.

This was the same type of irrational thinking that had told me it was a good idea to confront mutineers. The same type of thinking that had landed me here in the first place. I was exhausted. That was the only logical explanation for how I could look into this pirate's eyes and feel anything close to comfort. I wasn't thinking clearly. If I was going to survive this ordeal, I needed to push the image of the captain's eyes far, far out of my mind.

"Why?" I asked defensively.

"So I shall know what to call ye."

"Not to hunt down my family and demand ransom?"

"Ye have my word, lass," he sighed deeply and took both my hands in his. I didn't want to believe him, but I saw genuine sincerity in his stormy eyes.

I flinched at the contact but didn't pull away. I wish I could say I was trying to be brave, not show how scared I was of this whole situation. But if I was being honest, it was the first friendly touch I'd had in days. It felt nice. But risky. Like feeling the warm sun on your face, but knowing if you basked too long, you'd get burned.

"You can call me Sloane."

"Sloane," he echoed. I saw the smallest of smiles flash across his face.

He slowly pushed back my sleeves, exposing my blistered and raw wrists. Without explanation, he reached for the small glass bottle and poured what appeared to be oil into his palms. He rubbed his palms together then gingerly took hold of my wrists.

"Oil of chamomile." He massaged the oil tenderly into my wrists. It stung initially, but then soothed the burning sensation of chafed skin. After applying the oil, he wrapped my wrists one at a time in the linen strips.

As he worked, I inspected the foreign specimen before me. His face was striking with sharp angles in his jaw and cheekbones, lined with only a few days' worth of beard. The short stubble didn't hide his rich, sun-bronzed skin. His hair was a matching chestnut and fell to his shoulders. The top half was pulled back and tied with a leather strap; sun-bleached strips of caramel were mixed in with thin braids and twisted locks.

Handsome and fearsome at the same time.

Though markedly less fearsome, now that his face was cleaned of soot and he was wearing a fresh shirt.

To my utter surprise and mild rush of adrenaline, he took my foot into his lap and took off my shoe before reaching under my skirt to undo my stockings tied below my knee. I made a sharp intake of breath at his wandering hands. For a brief moment, I was going to slap him across the face for his boldness, but then he met my eyes. Those storm gray and steely blue eyes threatened to stop my heart once again.

He repeated the same process on my other leg, removing the shoe and stocking before tending to my ankle burns with the oil. All this without exchanging a single word. While he said nothing, I was at a loss for words. This moment felt intimate. It was certainly more intimate than any of my dates with good ol' Barney. I hoped the captain wouldn't notice the redness I was certain had crept onto my cheeks. I didn't want him to know how affected I was.

When he reached across to take my left ankle, I saw the side of his shirt bloom with red.

"You're bleeding!" I shouted, breaking the hypnotic tenderness.

He lifted his arm and twisted to see the blood for himself. "Ach, it's naught but a scratch...I'll go see the surgeon after this."

"Let me," I said. Without thinking, I reached out, my fingertips just touching where his shirt was tucked into his breeches. He cleared his throat and took a swift step back. *What was I thinking touching him like that?!* Clearly, I wasn't thinking at all. Seeing his wound, I acted out of instinct, nothing more.

"That's verra kind, lass. But I'll see to the surgeon, ye must be right tired after yer ordeal." Heat rushed up my chest and cheeks with humiliation at my heedless action.

"I am indeed." Mad and embarrassed, I shoved my makeshift bed of flour sacks and sails out the door. "Though I'd rather sleep on the floor than a bag of flour like a rat." I settled myself, curled up on the floor, my back to the captain.

I heard him lock my cell and instantly regretted my petty choice to reject the bedding. After sleeping on the hard wood for several days, my body would surely be grateful for any bit of cushion. Why did I let his rejection upset me like that? It's not like I actually wanted to care for him. I was acting a fool.

I looked up when his receding footsteps stopped. He was looking back in my direction. "Sleep well, my lady."

"Captain."

CHAPTER SEVEN

Unexpected Victories

The cabin boy returned the next morning with hot broth, a linen towel and some water to wash with. As Jonas unlocked the cell to allow the boy to bring the bucket in, I wondered if this was another thoughtful gesture on behalf of the captain.

I pushed away any thoughts of intrigue or flattery and reminded myself of the monster covered in others' blood I met on the other ship. No amount of chamomile oil could cover up who he really was—a captain of butchers. The man that tenderly cared for my delicate flesh was simply a mirage.

I thanked the boy and asked his name.

"Ye can call me Fish, ma'am." He bowed, nearly bringing his nose to his toes. "Yer servant, my lady."

"Fish?" I asked. He nodded. "Well, *Fish*, I thank you again."

That made him smile and rewarded me with another of his back breaking bows before scuttling away. *Hmm, Fish?*

Still reminded me more of a kitten with his shaggy copper hair and big, round eyes.

I set about tying the corners of my towel around the bars of my cell to create some semblance of privacy to make my toilette. I could see steam rising from both the broth and bucket of wash water and decided I'd much rather drink cold broth than bathe with cold water.

The warm water felt close to heaven, and I relished in the familiar comfort of a hot bath. Given that my stay had been laced up the back, there was only so much I could clean with the majority of my clothing still on, but I minded little.

• • •

I had a plan. It was far from perfect, and it was only half-formed, but if I didn't do something, *anything,* to solve this mess, I would lose my mind. In fact, maybe I already had because so far, my brilliant plan included threatening the scariest man I'd ever met with a butter knife.

Dear Lord, this was hopeless. I twirled the small knife I'd snuck from one of my meal platters and experimented pressing my thumb on the rounded tip. Dull. Utterly useless.

But it was my only plan, short of seducing the captain and convincing him to return the wine. And that was merely a thought experiment, there was absolutely zero chance of that happening. It's not that he wasn't nice to look at. In fact, he was shockingly handsome for a murderer and fit nothing into the ghoulish image of pirates in my head. His icy blue eyes still made a knot form in my stomach every time he looked at me. It was more the fact that, for him, having blood on his hands wasn't a metaphor.

I tried to tell myself that it was misplaced affection because he saved me from the man that first found me. But my mind still battled to determine who Captain Elliot Cross was. Was he the blood-soaked, savage pirate or was he the tender man who cared for my damaged wrists and ankles? Was he both? Was it even possible for those two men to coexist in one body?

I didn't know the answer and I didn't plan to be on this ship long enough to find out. It was time to set my plan in motion.

"Jonas, do you have keys for this?" I shook the metal door before doubling over with a pained scream. For such an oaf of a man, he was at the cell door incredibly quickly. His boyish eyes big and round, his brow creased with concern.

"No, ma'am." I knew he didn't have the keys, only the captain did. "But I'll go fetch the captain right away." Once more, I groaned and clutched my midsection for good measure as he barreled through the ship.

I didn't expect him to react so concerned to my apparent illness. I almost felt bad for tricking him. But how was I supposed to know a battle-hardened pirate would panic at the first sign of a little pain?

I actually expected it to take a performance of being nearly on my deathbed before he would take me seriously.

I heard the pounding of running feet and jingling keys and composed myself again. I leaned weakly against the bars and screwed up my face in a grimace.

"Captain," I said in a strained whisper. "I need to see the surgeon, I am very unwell. Please."

He inserted the key into the lock and paused. *Was he calling my bluff?*

"I'll bring him to ye." He pulled the key out and my stomach dropped. This wasn't a part of the plan. I didn't need the surgeon, I needed the captain to unlock the bloody cell door.

"No!" I shouted as he turned to leave. "Please, I cannot wait. Take me to him."

"Alright." I was antsy as he worked the lock and reminded myself of everything that was at stake. Even if my plan was idiotic and destined to fail, I had to at least try.

When he opened the cell door, I collapsed into him. His body was solid and hot against the bare skin of my chest that was left uncovered by my low neckline. And for a moment, I forgot about my plan, the wine and the pirate ship itself. He felt like a trusted shelter, his strength and protection unshakable.

But only for a moment.

I drew my knee up as hard and fast as I could between his legs. He shouted and stumbled back, and I took those precious few seconds to sprint in the direction Jonas had returned from with the empty wine crates.

The captain bellowed my name and I tried to speed up, but my legs burned from exertion after so little use the last several days.

I passed dozens of crates and barrels and other parcels, but none of it was my wine. Did they not take it all from the other ship? Was it just those two crates? Horror struck me as I realized I had just angered a very strong, very violent pirate over wine that may not even be on board.

The deeper into the ship I ran, the mustier the air got. The damp wood smelled like a shallow pond blooming with algae. A French word caught my eye and I exhaled in huge relief when I stopped to count the crates in front of me. Most, if not all, of the shipment was here.

Footsteps approached at an unhurried pace; he wasn't running after me. He was stalking me like a panther stalks a deer, slow and at ease with the confidence that he would come out on top, no need to rush.

I darted behind a tower of crates waiting, my heart beating so fast I was sure he could hear it.

He walked past my hiding spot and paused. Had the predator in him sensed my presence?

I gripped the knife. Its wooden handle felt puny in my hand when I looked at the captain's broad, capped shoulders. Even through his loose shirt, I could make out the powerful muscles that corded his back and arms.

Maybe I didn't have to go through with it. Maybe I could stay hidden until we reached land. Lord knows how many dark nooks and crannies there were on this ship. Perhaps we were even close, and I wouldn't have to hole out too long. But then what? It's not like I could sneak off board with hundreds of bottles of wine.

No, my current plan, no matter how flawed, was still my best chance.

I silently tiptoed out and closed the distance between myself and the captain's back. I pressed the tip of the knife to the nape of his neck. He didn't flinch.

"I want your word that you'll surrender the wine to me, *the rightful owner*, when we reach land."

"Or else?"

"Or I'll kill you." It felt like I had just signed my own death warrant, not his, with my words. Did people threaten pirate captains and survive?

"Ye'll have yer wine." *Did I hear that right?* My mouth hung open in suspended disbelief. Did it work? My destined-for-failure plan?

"Your word. Give me your word." I didn't know what a pirate's word was worth, but if he gave it, I would feel like the impossible had really happened.

"Ye have my word, the wine is yers." A weight the size of a buffalo lifted off my chest and for the first time since I was taken, I felt a sliver of hope...

In a blur, he spun around lightning fast, gripping my hand with the knife and wrapping it around me. He pinned my other arm behind me in between my back and his front. He forced my wrist to bend so I was holding the knife against my own throat.

I felt everything at once and nothing at the same time. His rock-hard body seared against me. My heart leaped to my throat and my body hummed with frightened anxiety. But concurrently, time stood still and all I could feel was the cool tip of the knife on the thin skin of my throat and the nearly unnoticeable sway of the ship on waves.

"Be careful with this thing, ye could hurt yerself." His breath tickled my neck and sent a rush of chills down my spine. The palm twisted behind me could feel the rippling muscle on his stomach when he spoke.

"And next time ye threaten someone with a blade, make sure it can actually break the skin." His lips brushed my ear and tension knotted between my legs. *What the hell was that about?* He must have felt whatever it was too, because the tension in between *his* legs pushed against the curve of my bottom.

Was my breathing slow and deep because I was scared for my life or because he held me tight against his body? Horrified by the very strong likelihood of the latter, I tried to twist out of his grip.

"Kill me or get your hands off me." He let me struggle for a few more seconds before releasing me with a chuckle.

"Ye got more brass than half my crew, my lady. Don't know many men who'd go looking for a fight they got no chance of winning." He was mocking me. My cheeks burned with annoyance.

"Well, you gave me your word, so I guess it worked." I tried to push past him, his body filling the narrow corridor created by towers of cargo on either side. "Get out of my—"

He rotated quickly and suddenly, pushing me up against a stack of crates, his palms flat on either side of my head. My pulse fluttered, my heart beating in my throat. I forced myself to meet his stormy gaze. They swallowed me whole like the ocean itself. I bit my lip to keep my breathing steady

He dragged the pad of his thumb over my bottom lip, loosening it out from under my teeth. I had no words, no witty retort, just the tingling sensation left from his touch. I was small and weak. And exhilarated. He could take me right here and I would be powerless to stop him.

"What do you want, Captain?" My voice was barely above a whisper. Was it an accusation? Or a plea? Even I didn't know.

His smoldering expression cooled, like he was coming back from a dream. His usual distant and cold look returned. He stepped back and let me walk away without ever answering my question.

Jesus, Mary, and Joseph.... My mind and body struggled to explain what had just happened. But they could agree on one thing—After all the events of the last few days, I was disgusted with myself for being so affected by being at the captain's mercy... thrilled even.

• • •

"Mistress Sloane?"

"Captain?" I responded from behind my makeshift bathing curtain I'd rehung after last night's confusing encounter. I had hoped out of sight, out of mind.

"I was wondering if ye'd like to accompany me on a walk?"

"A walk?" I poked my head around the curtain. "Yesterday you held a knife to my throat and now you want to go on a *walk?*"

"I'll remind ye that a knife was also held against my throat."

"Touché. But that doesn't mean I want to go anywhere with you." I dropped the corner of the curtain, letting it fall in front of his face.

A blade came jutting through the bars, piercing the fabric. He dragged his sword all the way down, cutting it in half, just connected at the top.

"What in God's name do you think you're doing!" Another stab and drag between the next set of bars. He continued tearing the fabric into strips until it dangled like a fringe. "Okay, okay, I will walk with you, just stop your little tantrum."

He gave me a sly corner smile, and as irritated as I was, I couldn't help but feel a pinch of giddiness at making him smile.

"Fish seems to be quite smitten with ye," he said while opening the cell door.

"Oh, was it him who brought me a hot meal and water? I thought it was you."

"Does it matter?"

"No," I spit out, I didn't want to give any hint that I hoped it was his doing. "Why is he called that anyway?"

"We found him, a few years past, in a barrel of salted fish." I widened my eyes at him in disbelief. "It's God's honest truth, my lady. We were almost two days into our voyage when Cook found him while prepping the noon meal. He was too scared or shy to tell us the full story then, but we figured it was one of two things."

He opened the door and I rose to join the captain on our "walk." I wasn't sure exactly what a walk in the middle of the ocean would include, but if it was even a little bit of fresh air, I was game.

"One, he purposefully snuck into the barrel to catch a free trip. Or two—the more likely, as I highly doubt a skittish child, like Fish, would intentionally put himself aboard a ship full of pirates—he climbed into the barrel to feed his hunger, closed the lid over himself so as not to get caught while feasting and accidentally fell asleep. Next thing he knows, he's inside a barrel of salted fish somewhere in the Caribbean."

"So, he got the name because he hitched a ride with some salty companions." I chuckled at the image.

"No, he's called Fish because he smelled like one for damn near a month after his wee adventure—you can imagine the stench, a few men were close to throwing him overboard."

I wrinkled my nose. "I'd much rather not submit my imagination to such a thought." Though he didn't say anything, I thought I caught another small smile.

When we reached the top deck, I simply stopped, closed my eyes, and appreciated the sensations. My first thought was how fresh and clean the sea air smelled compared to the dank mustiness below. The wind tickled my face and bits of hair that had fallen out of my plait played in the wind.

We proceeded to the rails, and I peered over the edge. The water battered the side of the ship and the clear, blue sky dropped diamonds in the folds of the waves. Looking at the expanse in front of me, I felt dizzyingly confused. Anytime I thought about the fact that I was literally surrounded by pirates, I was nearly paralyzed with fear. But in that very moment, with the horizon stretching out endlessly, I felt a calm I couldn't explain. Perhaps it was the familiarity of water. Whether it was the port at New Bern or the middle of the Caribbean, the water didn't care if you were a pirate or a saint. It was a calming constant.

"There's the Cap'n's whore!" Spinning around, a face jerked me from my peaceful gazing and sent a rush of panic through my limbs. Even with two pronounced black eyes, now fading to shades of yellow and blue, I recognized him immediately, the first pirate to find me aboard the mutineer's ship. Our eyes met and it felt as if a bucket of ice melt was dumped over my head. His face remained passive, unmoved if not for the slightest leer. "Cunt," he spat at me from across the deck.

I hadn't even realized I had put a hand on the railing to steady myself until I felt a hand on mine. I jumped at the contact, but the captain didn't remove his hand. My knuckles were white from gripping the banister.

"He'll no' bother ye again, lass." I looked up to him and despite everything inside me begging me to run, jump overboard, anything to put distance between me and my attacker, I felt reassured and protected. *There it was again!* My girlish subconscious trying to make this violent pirate into something gentle and kind. I mentally kicked myself.

"You locked me in a cage! You're no better than him, don't you dare try to defend me." I shook his hand off. "I can protect myself just fine." I couldn't let him get inside my head this way. He was a dangerous man, not some white knight. It was a constant whiplash of emotion being near him.

"Why did you stop him? I saw what you did to that crew. After all that bloodshed, I'm surprised you'd find moral objection to rape."

"A woman's lovin' is to be given, not taken." His long hair also blew in the wind and the caramel strands were more golden in the sunlight. *What did a pirate captain know about love?*

"But—" I needed to prove to myself that the monster was there, behind the angular face and soul-wrenching eyes. "You're a bloody pirate for Christ's sake! You take what isn't yours—you murder, you plunder. It's what you do."

"In my world,"—he swept his arm to take in the entirety of the ship and the crew—"in this world, where there is no law and order, there is only honor. Killin', thievin', raidin'—there's honor in that depending on where ye stand. But rape? Nay, there's no honor in that." It was like someone telling me the sky is green and grass is blue. A pirate captain speaking of honor and moral codes left my brain feeling off-balance; it was paradoxical.

He wrapped his hand around my fingers. "Walk with me," he said, still holding my hand in his. Something about his warm and strong hand around mine made me feel balanced again.

And I hated it.

• • •

I stopped counting after our third lap around the deck. Most of the time we walked in silence. Being able to stretch my legs and take more than just a few steps felt amazing.

I had never spent time on the deck of a vessel of this size before and curiously watched the crew climbing, pulling and shouting seemingly without reason. Like watching ants scattering in and out of an ant hill. You see nothing but apparent chaos and dysfunction. Though in reality, each minuscule step an ant takes, and every speck of dirt moved is part of a finely-tuned symphony. And each part is critical to the survival of the rest.

"Sloane," the Captain's voice broke me from my daydream of ants, "I'd like to show you to your cabin."

"I wouldn't necessarily call a locked cell a cabin, Captain."

"I told you that was only temporary. Arrangements had to be made."

We descended back down into the belly of the ship to the crew's quarters, weaving in and out of hammocks. Most hung limp and empty, but a few held sleeping sailors. Wrapped in the hammock like a babe in a swaddle, they didn't look so rugged and brutal. In fact, as I passed their dozing heads, watching their faces flitter with small movements as they dreamed, I almost felt the desire to pet their hair.

Eventually, we came to a door with mermaids among waves carved into the wood. The captain unlocked the door and held it open for me.

The cabin was tiled with ivory and iridescent shells. Four lanterns hung in the corners of the room with delicately forged metal screens in a lace-like pattern that made the fire dance through the room. At the center back was a bold and handsome desk mounted to the floor and littered with rolls and sheets of parchment. To the right, hung a bed with no legs.

The mattress sat upon a flat, wood pallet that hung from thick ropes tied to each corner. The bedding wasn't impressive by my mother's standards at home but was royal in comparison to the stained and tattered blankets and hammocks the crew slept on. One, long stuffed pillow stretched from side to side on top of a quilt made of purple cloth. It looked so inviting, I couldn't help but run my fingers over the amethyst fabric. To say this an improvement from my previous accommodations was a gross understatement.

"I'm glad you like it." He looked at me with a smile. "This is the captain's cabin, but it'll be where you stay now."

The smile that just seconds before I found charming, now reminded me of Captain Baker's lecherous grin. Of course, this savage pirate captain was not hiding a polite and caring gentleman. He was merely playing a role, letting me drop my guard until he could make his true intentions clear.

"I will be no man's whore." I took a step closer to him. "I don't give a damn whether you're a pirate captain or His Majesty, the bloody King." I was shocked to hear the growl in my own voice. I was so sick of being forced around by men who thought they owned me. I was sick of my parents trying to marry me off. I was sick of Lord Barnaby Thomas and his patronizing proposal. And I was absolutely sick and tired of pirates and mutineers.

As if moving of its own volition, my hand slapped across his cheek. My hand stung and he barely batted an eye. This man might truly be made of stone. I flexed my aching fingers. For a tense moment, the captain didn't say anything, and I expected retaliation any second. I braced for impact, honestly too mad to be scared.

He let out a loud and husky laugh. "As much I'd love to take a bonny lass like ye—" His words made me instantly blush. Did he just call me beautiful? *Not that I care a single bit what he thinks,* I reminded myself. "I dinna think I'll be verra successful on the other side of that door."

"You mean you're giving me your sleeping quarters and expecting nothing in return?"

"Aye." He took a step toward me, closing the gap between us to just a foot or two. *What was he doing?* He was close enough I could smell his masculine mix of sweat and sea water. My gaze shifted from his piercing blue eyes to the sharp line of his nose, only interrupted by a small zig where it must have been broken in the past.

A good head taller, he looked down at me. I felt his eyes wander from my tousled and messily plated golden hair to my breasts still on immodest display, having been unable to adjust the tight laces myself, and down to the hem of my dress as if he was imagining what it might be hiding. His smoldering assessment of me made my breathing deepen, which to my great embarrassment, only made my pushed-up breasts rise and fall more obviously.

My eyes found his lips, a handsome ocher color that formed a strong line, like every other angle on his face. He parted his lips, and I could sense what was coming next. He was about to kiss me, and I wasn't sure I would try to stop him...

"Though I wouldn't mind if ye found some way to make yerself useful on board until we make land." He gave me a playful look and coy smile as if he knew what I had been expecting.

I could do nothing but let out a weak chuckle and nod my head like a bobbing idiot. What foolish recess of my mind did I just go to, to think he, a *bloody pirate captain,* was about to kiss me! I was even more disturbed when a part of me was disappointed when he didn't.

To distract myself from my confusing thoughts about his mouth, I asked the first question that came to mind while I strolled to his desk across the room to put distance between us. "Why?"

"Idle hands are the devil's workshop." He crossed to the far side of the cabin where a large cabinet was built out the wall. "Plus, ye'll grow right bored without a job to keep ye busy, and I dinna want anyone under my watch to throw themselves into the ocean because they were literally bored to death."

"I mean why move me from a cage to your own captain's quarters?" I asked. I didn't believe there was nothing more to this. Surely a pirate captain would have more sinister motives than simple hospitality.

"After a raid is no good time for a lady to be meandering aboard a pirate ship." He leaned back against the cabinet and crossed his legs at the ankles. I envied how relaxed he appeared, while I was over here reeling, my mind and body in a heated debate on whether or not I wished he had kissed me. "You see, men are wounded—or dead—and need urgent tending. That alone is a messy situation. Then add in the organization and storing of the prize and any new recruits, you got people running 'round like they got a lightning bolt up their ass."

I circled the desk, skimming the parts of parchment that were visible while he talked. "And then there's all the men that are still roarin' with fighting spirit. Their hearts are poundin', they can still smell their enemy's blood and are shaking with the excitement and fear that come from boarding a prize ship." I swallowed hard remembering the gory scene. He let that image sink in before continuing, more cautious and softer in the way he spoke. "After my man attacked ye, I knew I had to protect ye while the men cooled down. But I couldn't possibly stay by yer side—my attention was needed in a hundred different places."

I looked up at him remembering the first time I saw his face, covered in black soot and blood. I recalled the face of a monster, but here in front of me was a man only thinking of protecting a woman he'd never met while his crew recovered. Meeting his ocean eyes from across the small room, a small flutter danced in my stomach. Each time I tried to paint a picture of who Captain Elliot Cross was, he would say or do something that wiped my canvas blank again.

"While I appreciate your efforts on account of my safety..." Trying to ignore the butterflies in my stomach, I redirected the conversation to something I was much more comfortable with, "Unfortunately, you just won't be profitable if you go by these numbers." In front of me on the desk was a leather-bound ledger with messily logged goods and plans for dividing their worth.

Having piqued his interest, he came around the desk to stand behind me, looking over my shoulder. I began to point out the errors I'd spotted. "For starters, your pricing for tobacco and indigo is way off. You may have once been able to fetch that price, but not anymore with the plantations only becoming more and more efficient with the crops."

I could see him nod in consideration in my peripheral and could feel the slight breeze of his breath on my neck. It instantly propelled me back to yesterday when he held me flush against him. Feeling myself getting distracted again by ridiculous thoughts of his body on mine, I continued with the modest topic at hand.

"That alone makes all your numbers and shares useless because you're working with the wrong gross. But here,"—I pointed to the bottom of the page—"you've created a cost per share by dividing the net profit by the number of men aboard. But you failed to take into account the men that get double shares and the shares set aside for 'compensation'— whatever that is."

"Injury and death compensation." Hearing his husky voice, but not being able to see him, just sense him, behind me made me squirm inside. "If a man gets injured or dies, compensation will be paid to him or his family."

"That's shockingly thoughtful for a pirate crew." I turned around to face him, not being able to stand his teasing, hovering presence any longer.

"On this ship, we're family. No one is above anyone else." I'd offended him. I could tell in his clipped tone. And while I obviously didn't usually care about offending men, that wasn't my intention *this* time.

"I meant no disrespect, I just didn't know." His eyes softened and I relaxed a bit.

"Och, I know ye didn't. Most people don't know a fraction of what goes on on these ships. They just assume the worst." *People like me.*

"Did ye know that we vote on the articles of the ship and even hold elections for positions like Captain and Quartermaster? Ye'd be hard pressed to find a military or merchant ship whose crew has half as much voice as us pirates."

I realized that's all I'd ever wanted at Sinclair Trading, a voice. I wanted not only to be heard but to have my voice mean something, to lead to action.

He nodded to the ledger. "But about this mess, our quartermaster was killed when we boarded. A bullet got him just as he was climbing over next to me. He was a good man and a fair quartermaster—did a fine accounting job too." His face was a stoic display of the loss, he clearly thought highly of the man. "But me? I can barely use a quill. And I'm no' my finest with numbers, but ye seem to have a good head for them, aye?"

He said it like it was a good thing. Lord Thomas would no sooner talk finances with me than he would admit to being a spoiled man child. It was nice to be seen in that way.

"I'll make myself useful by cleaning up your books and when we get to land, I'll make sure you get a good price," I said confidently, already feeling more comfortable being in a familiar environment with numbers, inventory and trade.

"I've never known a lady with a mind for business."

"Congratulations, Captain, you have now." He raised his brows at me as if expecting me to continue. "And I suppose I can also help the surgeon with minor injuries and lend a hand with mending those holey rags your crew calls clothes, if nursing and sewing would appeal more to your manly sensibilities."

The corner of his mouth turned up in a smile. "That suits me just fine, Mistress Sloane."

• • •

Now that I was no longer confined to a cell, I joined the crew in their living quarters for the evening meal. This night though, I was going to eat alone in my new cabin, but as I headed that way, the captain grabbed my hand.

"No, come eat with us." He gently led me by the hand but dropped it when we got closer to the men. When I was connected to him, I felt tethered and safe. But as soon as his hand let go, it was as if I'd been dropped into chummed waters. He gave me a small look of encouragement. Perhaps he was trying to show me that I could handle being around the men without him.

And I was inclined to believe him as we sat down on small rum barrels at a hanging table. The men looked my way but didn't stare. No one made the lewd remarks I had expected, and a few even greeted me with a nod.

If it wasn't for my bandaged wrists and the constant sway of the table, I could almost imagine I was back at the Dogwood Inn.

A call for the captain came down the companionway. He got up to leave, but then turned back and met my eyes. "I'll be back shortly, ye'll be alright?"

"Of course." I was equal parts warmed that he was thinking of my safety, *again,* and annoyed that he was acting like I was a lost, little girl. He took the steps two at a time and quickly disappeared.

Immediately the hairs on the back of my neck stood up, I was surrounded. My heart raced knowing that there were at least twenty pirates behind me. I narrowed my eyes on my meal, biscuit and dried pork, and tried to tune out the whispered voices. I couldn't make out their words, but I couldn't help but assume they were about me.

"Ye must be a good lay if the Cap'n gives ye his cabin." The slick drawl made me spin around on the barrel I was using as a seat. It was the man who assaulted me on the other ship. I ground my teeth together, not knowing how to respond.

Like a viper, his hand shot out and grabbed a fistful of my hair. He yanked my head back, so I was forced to look up into his hate-filled, bloodshot eyes. "I shoulda fucked ye when I had the chance." His rancid breath and the tugging on my hair made my eyes water.

The sound of heavy boots descending the steps made him release my hair but not before he growled, "And don't think I won't another time."

If my heart was racing before, it was now threatening to burst through my chest.

He walked away the same moment the captain returned. The captain looked at the man and then back at me. His jaw clenched and his voice lowered to a deep and gritty timber. "What did McDonald say to ye?"

"Nothing." He must have noticed my eyes were watering and I hated the thought that he took them as tears. "I'm fine." My voice shook slightly, and he looked at me questioningly but didn't push the issue.

He sat back down and resumed his meal, but I just pushed my pork around my plate. An anger boiled up in me that burned through my chest and cheeks. The one thing I despised most was feeling pathetic.

I couldn't stand the thought that all these men saw me as a frail, blubbering flower they could stomp on as they pleased. Feeling defenseless like that made my stomach knot.

"Sloane?" The captain was looking down at the table and I realized I was stabbing my fork into the wooden table, my fist gripped so tightly my knuckles were white.

"Give me your blade."

"What? Sloane, what happened with McDonald when I was gone?"

"Didn't I tell you to let me fight my own battle?" Venom laced my words. "Now, give me your damn blade." He handed it over with a look somewhere between reluctant and curious.

I made a straight line to McDonald who was sitting a few tables down with his back to me. Emboldened and fired up, I fisted his hair and returned the favor of yanking his head back. But instead of mere threats, I pressed the captain's blade to his throat. Hard. Hard enough to draw a little blood and make his eyes widen. He needed to know how serious I was.

The other men at the table stood up but didn't make a move against me. *Good.*

"Listen up!" I shouted, though it wasn't necessary as by now everyone was silent, eyes on me. "In the past days, I've been betrayed, kidnapped, beaten, chained, ransomed, and assaulted. *I am at my limits.* And I will not tolerate any more crap from pieces of shit like this." I tugged on McDonald's head emphasizing my point.

"Now, does anyone here have a problem with that?" My voice may have been shaking before, but it wasn't anymore. It came out strong and confident and my pride welled. I knew I wasn't the easy prey they thought I was.

I scanned the hold. A lot of the men's expressions were a mix and too hard to discern. But others, I could easily recognize. Some were entertained like this was an amusing show. Some were surprised as if I was suddenly naked. But most of their faces were lined with newfound respect.

When no one said anything in protest, I withdrew the blade and shoved McDonald's head into his plate of food.

I handed the captain his blade. He looked at me expecting an explanation as he wiped the small bit of blood off.

"You said next time I threaten someone with a knife, I better make sure the blade can break the skin." He shook his head and his throaty laugh warmed me to the core.

Sitting back down, I didn't feel the same nervousness with my back to the men I had felt just minutes before.

CHAPTER EIGHT

New Rhythms

The night I stood up to McDonald was a turning point for me and the crew. Over the next week, I fell into a comfortable rhythm on board.

Each morning with Fish's help, I would gather the day's rations that I had calculated the night before. He had become my skittish shadow and I was becoming quite fond of the little lad.

The two of us would bring the food stuff from storage to the galley. The cook was a weathered old man who only pretended to be crotchety. He would huff and puff about the terrible supplies he was forced to work with and the "ungrateful bastards" referring to the crew. But I would catch glimpses of him whistling while he worked and smiling pleased after tasting the day's soup. He even lit up like a proud grandfather as he patiently taught Fish the fastest way to peel a potato or how to brown onions for the most flavor.

He could huff and puff all he wanted, but I saw the joy of an artist in his studio.

After our drop at the galley, I would return to my cabin. Outside my door was a basket filled with various tattered items of clothing. Throughout the day and night shifts, men would drop off anything that needed mending. And my Lord, one would think they spent all day fighting tigers by the way they were tearing up their clothes. I honestly don't know how they had anything but threads to wear before I arrived.

If the weather was nice, I would haul the basket up to the top deck and sew in the sun. My little shadow usually helped—unless Cook needed him—and proved to be surprisingly competent with a needle and thread.

The captain would saunter past and make a joke about my feminine nature being put to good use. I would come back with something about poking his eye out with a needle and he would give me a wink that made me glad I was already sitting down.

One day after our usual banter, I muttered "bloody devil" as the captain walked away. Fish was instantly on his feet offering to fight him for me. It took all my self-control to not laugh at his boyish gallantry and instead said, "You are quite the gentleman, Fish. But there will be no fighting today."

I watched as the captain mingled with his crew and always found it curious how quickly the men seemed to straighten up when he came near. Though it wasn't out of fear that made them stand to attention. He clearly held their respect and they wanted to please him. He could break up a quarrel by simply approaching, not pulling the brawlers apart or shouting to stop. He led with confidence and in return the crew had confidence in him.

The sun and fresh air were an obvious appeal to working on the deck, but I couldn't ignore the appeal of watching the captain. My heart picking up pace anytime his gaze caught mine from across the ship. And I liked to think he liked watching me too. For he seemed to be paying attention to my progress and always came around every time I was finishing up my mending for the day.

The first few days, he would come over to me with a proffered hand and say, "Walk with me." But by the end of the week, he would just offer his hand without a word. And I always took it.

In the evening, I would pay a visit to the surgeon and help where I could. It was mostly cuts, rope burns and pulling massive splinters from flesh, but occasionally someone would fall from a net and break an arm or pull a muscle lifting heavy sails or barrels.

As days passed, I found the men less intimidating. It probably had something to do with seeing them bleed from cuts and bruise from falls. Proving they were made of the same mortal flesh as me.

Once the evening meal was ready, everyone but the working shift would gather in the living quarters. Food was hungrily slopped up and then the whiskey and ale were poured. It could have been any pub in the world if you ignored the fact that we were floating somewhere in the middle of the ocean.

Men would start playing dice, gambling away their next day's rations in the absence of silver. The few men that could hold a tune would lead a chorus of drunk, tone-deaf pirates in songs that reminded them of home. Here and there a snoring head would doze on a tabletop, passed out from exhaustion or ale or a combination of the two.

Fish would make rounds clearing plates and finishing off what was left in the passed-out men's mugs. He would always circle back to me, his little body limp and tired from a long day's work, swaying slightly from the stolen ale. He would settle down on a bench next to me and fall asleep with his head in my lap, while I petted his auburn mop of hair.

A comfortable rhythm indeed.

• • •

"Mistress, Mistress!" Fish came bursting on to the top deck where I had been journaling on the banister. He was out of breath, his usually unruly hair even more disheveled. And in the center of his chest was a dark cherry red swath of blood, paired with smears on his cheeks and arms.

Instantly, I dropped to my knees, my journal nearly falling into the ocean and began tapping his scrawny body from head to toe, trying to find the source of the blood.

"It's not me who's hurt, my lady. Come quick, he's asking for you." And with that he was off racing back below deck with me scurrying to keep up.

I could hear the screams of agony before we reached the surgery. Fish flung the door open, and I ran in before coming to an abrupt halt before the table.

Doc was urgently shuffling through his supplies while a young crew member named Solomon lay on his back on the table with two other men holding his shoulders down. Other than the typical filth and sweat that coated every man's face and shirt, there was nothing wrong with his upper half. It was his lower limb that made my stomach churn. His left pant leg had been cut up the middle and torn open to reveal the bone protruding from his shin.

"Dear heavenly father..." I muttered under my breath.

"Mistress Sloane." I was surprised to hear Solomon address me directly. "Thank ye for coming"

"You—you asked for me?" I didn't have much experience but having been acting as Doc's apprentice the last two weeks, I had assumed it was him who had sent Fish for me.

"Yes, I need to make arrangements for my share of the prize and injury compensation if I am to die.

"Uh, okay, I'll go get the captain."

"No, Mistress, it's your job as quartermaster." *Me, quartermaster?* Solomon's forehead was becoming slicker with sweat from exertion and his face was paling from blood loss. I figured I could be whatever he needed me to be. Quartermaster, Queen of England, it didn't matter as long as it eased his mind in this moment.

"Right, of course." I looked around for a parchment and quill. "Tell me what happened," I said to Solomon, then signaled to Fish that I needed a quill.

"I was fetching a few planks to repair the crow's nest. But something must not have been secured right, because when I pulled out the planks, one of them barrels came loose and knocked me flat on my back, crushing my leg here." His voice shook at points, his face tensed with concentration as he focused on getting words out despite unfathomable pain.

"Okay, and Solomon, tell me about your family."

"My daughter, ah my angel,"—for a split second his forehead relaxed at the thought of his little girl—"now, she stays with her grandmother, but she gets my share of the prize, aye?"

I took his sweaty palm that had been gripping the edge of the table. "What's she like?" He squeezed my hand.

"Blonde hair like her mum. Eyes so blue, it makes ye wanna cry, it does." He smiled. "And she's a real saint, eh? Don't know how she got it with me as her father, but she's real kind, likes animals too. Even tries to rescue the mice the cat catches." He laughed and it was such a pleasant sound in the gruesome setting. I felt my eyes prick with tears.

"Now, you're gonna be just fine, okay? Doc here is gonna fix you right up, better than new." Doc looked over at me with a nod. He was ready. "So, when you walk off this ship, where will you go to find her?"

"Her gran lives just past the Dunmore plantation—Mistress Sylvia Prescott is her name."

"Mistress Sloane, it's time for you to go." Doc looked at me and then turned to Solomon. "Son, I gotta set this bone now, drink up." He put a small glass bottle to his lips and Solomon let it slide down this throat.

I started to leave, patting Solomon's hand in farewell, but he held on tighter, pulling me back. "Will ye stay with me, my lady?" His voice broke and I could tell he was holding back tears. How scared he must be, even for a battle-seasoned pirate.

"I'm here." I firmly planted my feet and squeezed his hand back. "I'm here."

Solomon's eyes drooped from the laudanum and Doc told the other two men to hold him still. Doc placed his hand decisively on either side of the protruding shin bone. Solomon gasped at the pressure and crushed my fingers in response.

A strap of leather was placed between Solomon's teeth. "Bite down, boy."

• • •

I straightened back over the edge of the ship and wiped my mouth with a torn piece of linen taken from the surgery. The acidic taste of vomit coated my tongue, and Solomon's screams as Doc shoved his shattered bone back under his bloodied flesh still rang in my ears.

By some miracle, I held it together until Doc was finished splinting Solomon's leg. Solomon passed out from the pain and drugs. But the instant it was over, I made record time to the top deck.

I felt a hand on my lower back and started at the surprise contact. Over my shoulder stood the captain, shirtless and sweaty in the hot, Caribbean sun. A lump formed in my throat at his bronzed chest: it looked soft, like suede, with tiny blond hairs catching the sunlight.

I forced myself to look him in the eyes and not lower. "Do you know what I learned today?" I said accusatory. He raised his eyebrows. "That I'm apparently the bloody quartermaster of this damn pirate ship." I kicked the wood siding.

Rippling, golden ab muscles that made me want to reach out and touch them be damned, I wanted to go home. *Now.* Before I had to witness another man's extremities being reattached to his body for Christ's sake.

"I want to go home. No, I *need* to go home! Please just drop me off at the nearest port, I don't care where—I'll figure it out, but I want off this ship! Do you hear me?" He continued to stare at me, almost in amusement, which only made me angrier. "I just came from watching Doc literally push someone's bone back into their body. I held his hand while he screamed and came in and out of consciousness from the pain. I was nearly raped by one of your men and have been pretending like you all didn't just slaughter an entire crew a week ago!" I let out a heavy exhale. "I don't even belong on this ship, let alone serve as the goddamn quartermaster." I rested my elbows on the banister and buried my face in my hands, exasperated.

He began to say something, but I wasn't done. "What happens if you don't come out on top at the next raid? Huh? Will I just be kidnapped again? On to the next!" I threw my hands in the air before pounding my fists on his chest. "Huh? What then? I want off this bloody *fucking* ship!" My eyes stung with hot tears.

He covered my fists with his hands, flattening my palm against his chest. His skin was hot from the beating sun. My hand was like hot candle wax on his skin, making me want to melt into him. A chill ran up my spine despite the heat. "I will see ye safely home." His heart pounded under my palm at pace with my own. "Ye have my word." The corner of his mouth turned up. "I agree ye've been onboard too long—ye're startin' to sound like a pirate."

Laughter broke the intense moment. "Oh bloody hell." I rolled my eyes with a sigh and a smile.

CHAPTER NINE

Honor

"You said to me once that there is honor in killing and stealing depending on where you stand, what did you mean?"

We were sitting around a table for the evening meal. It was a rough day at sea and the hanging tables swung more than usual. I had to keep my hand wrapped around my mug to stop the ale from sloshing out. Most men were already in their hammocks, having worked hard to keep the ship on course in the choppy water. But some remained playing cards and getting in arguments over who was cheating, a nightly occurrence.

"Look 'round ye," he said. "These are the men discarded by society. They've been told their whole life they're worthless. They aren't given fancy educations and family businesses to inherit." I swallowed. He was describing me to a tee. "Instead, they're told to fight for their survival and then locked up and called monsteres when they do." How many times had I used the word monsters to describe pirates myself?

"So, when ye find a world that treats everyone equal, where ye get to keep the fruit of yer blood and sweat, ye stay," he continued.

"But you're just stealing someone else's fruit, not growing your own."

"Och, the goods we take are usually produced by the exploited poor or slaves, either way it's not a result of the bourgeoisies' hard work." He did have a point. My father was the rare exception of a merchant who didn't manage everything from the distance of his plush, comfortable estate. It took him decades of working alone before he finally hired Malcolm.

"Okay, let's say I understand a *little* of the stealing. How is there honor in killing? The crews on prize ships are innocent." The memory of Charlie Fraser's body bleeding out flashed in my mind.

"Believe it or not, we don't go 'round killin' people for sport. Heck, ninety percent of the time we take a prize, not a drop of blood is shed."

"Ha! You expect me to believe that? When I first met you, you were covered head to toe in blood." *And so was the rest of his crew.*

"There's still that one time out of ten. When a ship's captain choses pride over survival. Like that foolish oaf who took ye." I couldn't help but notice he bristled protectively when talking about my kidnapping and the man responsible.

"So, are they just supposed to give you whatever you want?"

"If they're smart, they will." He was so matter-of-fact and confident that I found myself agreeing with him. If you could leave a pirate raid with not a single scratch, why wouldn't you? "Most captains even keep specific cargo for when they're boarded, so they have something to give us, and we'll be on our merry way."

"You make it sound so cordial." I'd seen people riot over taxes and here he's telling me ship captains just hand over a treasure chest as the cost of doing business in pirate territory.

"We've done enough fightin' and killin' to make the black flag mean something. When ships see it, they know they will be boarded. It's up to them to choose if they live."

My time with the pirates so far had done a lot to dismiss a lot of my preconceived notions about their innate evilness. Jonas was like a five-year-old in a man's body, sweet and caring if not the sharpest spoon in the drawer. Solomon was like any other father who thought of his daughter as a princess and only wanted to do well by her. Speaking of, Solomon had gotten through the initial phase of fever and Doc seemed confident he would heal just fine if he kept on this trajectory, perhaps with a slight limp.

Then there was Hank, the boatswain, who liked to prank his crew mates on the daily but was always first to offer a hand when someone needed help. Josiah, one of the few literate men on board, read books by candlelight each night, and men gathered round to listen. Mickey, a deckhand, despite being the runt of the crew often started his already grueling, long shifts early to give a struggling mate much needed rest.

Living among them, I had obviously learned they weren't killing for breakfast, noon, and dinner but hearing the captain explain it hit differently. It was uncomfortable challenging my lifelong beliefs.

Part of me wanted to see a monster in the captain. I thought maybe if I did, I wouldn't fall asleep wondering what it would be like if he was next to me. Maybe then, our afternoon walks on deck wouldn't be the thing I looked forward to most in the day.

My thoughts were out of my control, like they belonged to someone else. My body wasn't my own when the lightest touch from him sent waves through my body. Being in his presence, I wanted it to burn like hot, glowing metal. But instead, it felt like the comforting warmth of falling asleep in front of the hearth.

The more I felt myself inexplicably drawn to him, the more I wanted to be repelled. In a way, I think I felt guilty. Likening any type of friendship with pirates was a betrayal to my father, like spitting on his brother's grave.

The emotional weight of witnessing Solomon's surgery rested on me heavily. He'd put a trust in me I didn't ask for. Apparently, the whole crew had. I'd been fighting so hard against accepting these men and yet they had accepted me. Even after I threatened to slit their crew mate's throat. Granted, McDonald was already not a crowd favorite.

"Hey, where'd ye go?" A hand placed on my knee under the table snapped me back from my internal debate. The captain lightly squeezed my knee, sending a sweet warmth up my legs. I clenched my inner thighs and looked up at him.

"Just plotting my escape from a pirate ship." His hand didn't leave my thigh like he was trying to keep my attention on him.

"Well, ye'll get yer chance very soon. O'Brien spotted the prize we've been huntin'. We'll be boarding her in the morning."

"No." I shook his hand off and stood up. Talking about and actually being an accomplice to a raid were two very different things. "I won't be a part of that."

He laughed. "Well, it's not really up to ye, lass."

"But if I'm supposedly the quartermaster of this bloody crew, I get a say."

"I seem to remember ye quite colorfully rejecting that title." His eyes held an amused darkness. Like he was threatening me to deny him but also enjoying seeing me flustered.

"Ugh, I'm going to bed." I started walking away. When he started following me, I shot him a glare. "Good night, Captain."

But he kept following me. His presence burned my back, but I refused to acknowledge him.

I got to my door but stopped without opening it and spun around.

"I get it. You're gonna do what you do tomorrow, kill, thieve, raid, and there's nothing I can do to stop it. Doesn't mean I have to like it."

"My God, woman, do ye have amnesia or are ye just deaf?" *What the hell did that mean?* I stepped close to him, my chin lifted to look up at him.

"I won't be a part of it."

"Did I no' just explain to ye that there'll be no fightin'? Did I no' just tell ye that we'll walk off that ship with the prize and not a single drop of blood will be shed?" He also took a step forward, forcing me to take one back. I knew this argument had little to do with the actual raid and much more to do with me feeling like I was getting pulled deeper and deeper into his world.

He took another step forward until my back hit the door behind me. He put one hand on my hip and one under my chin, forcing me to meet his hardened, stormy gaze

"I'll remind ye, I'm the captain of this ship and ye'll do as I say." His hand pressing on my hip caused a not unpleasant ripple through my body but when he came even closer and pinned me with his pelvis, I thought my heart would literally stop.

My breath became ragged, and I could tell he had to put in effort to keep his steady too. Having his body flush against my back was nothing compared to this extreme closeness while looking into his eyes.

"Do ye understand me?" I could feel his husky voice like a vibration in my chest. Breathless, I nodded. "Say it." He dragged his fingers that were under my chin up my jawline, and in that moment, I think I would have said anything he wanted me to say.

"You're the captain," His touch was sweet and caressing, but his demeanor demanded respect and fear. I hated how much the combination lit a pulsing flame between my legs.

"Aye, I am."

Like running into a brick wall, a sickening realization hit me—I wasn't trying to run away from the monster inside the captain, I was running away from my undeniable attraction to the monster.

CHAPTER TEN

Surrender

"Fire!" The captain's command rang in my ear but was quickly drowned out by the roar of the cannon. As soon as the first warning shot was fired, two men began rapidly hoisting up the black.

Seeing the flag blowing in the wind gave me chills. This ship's flag featured a long cutlass sword dripping with white drops of blood. A fitting insignia given it mimicked McDonald's sword the first time I saw him.

Another cannon boomed and on cue, the men jumped into action. Strapping on holsters, loading pistols, sharpening blades, preparing to fight.

"This seems like an awful lot of artillery to not be fighting..." I posed to the captain who was standing next to me overseeing the men.

"Aye, well we got a reputation to protect. If we showed up with roses, they wouldn't hand a thing over."

Fish dashed around with a basket of charcoal from the galley, offering it to men to paint their faces. I'd heard of Indians in the colonies painting their faces for battle and I could see why. With just a little soot, these already intimidating men transformed into downright terrors.

The clang of metal filled the air as men warmed up their sword work with each other. We were quickly closing the distance between the two ships and teams of men hustled to prepare the nets and gang plank for boarding. My chest tightened and anxious energy gripped my stomach. I wanted to go below deck and hide, pretend this wasn't happening, but for some reason I felt that if I looked away, this whole situation would erupt.

Fish came up to me and the captain and the captain pulled out a small, charred piece of wood.

"It's good luck to have a lady paint ye for battle." He held out the stick. I didn't believe him but took it anyway.

"Okay, uh what do I do?" It felt like I was about to summon a demon.

"Anything ye like, my lady." A faint smile pulled on his lips, and I had the urge to freeze time. His cool, soulful eyes locked on mine, his face warmed by the hint of a smile.

I rubbed the charred stick across my fingertips until they were thoroughly covered in soot. I was about to wipe it on his face but paused when I realized I'd never touched his face before. Suddenly it felt all too intimate.

"Well don't take all morning. I got places to be, aye?"

"Right, of course." Remembering the soot when I first met him, I dragged my fingertips from his temple to the opposite jaw in a wide diagonal band. My hand hovered on his jaw, almost cupping his cheek. He must have sensed my anxiety because he gently removed my hand, clutched it between his, and said, "Dinna fash yerself, my lady—this willna be like the last one."

Embarrassed at my outward display of weakness, I shook his hands off. "I'm not scared. I just don't want to end up going from *quartermaster* to bloody captain if something happens to you."

"Captain, we're ready," a man hollered as the two ships were now only fifty feet apart.

"Go, you're needed." I shoved him by the shoulder. He strode across the deck and fell in line next to his men, crouched behind the railing as the two ships grew even closer.

When the two vessels looked so close they would collide, a few men at each end of the ship and a pair in the middle stood and threw nets with grappling hooks that caught on the broadside of the other ship.

"Why have they no' struck their colors?" Doc came up beside me, his voice a mix of concern and surprise.

"What do you mean?"

"Their flags, they're still hoisted." He didn't look at me, just straight ahead at the men who were readying their guns and unsheathing swords. "They havena surrendered."

"*What?*" As if in response, the entire crew seemed to release a giant roar as they leaped up and over the railing. They shot their bodies across the gap like squirrels, clinging to the hanging net on the prize ship.

Instantaneously, dozens of gun barrels sprung up from the opposing ship and fired. My stomach dropped, my pulse raced, and my head swam.

It was happening again.

There wasn't going to be anything peaceful about this.

All the smoke from the gunshots clouded the crew and I couldn't make anything out visually. I could only hear the fight rage, like bad déjà vu.

As if nailed to the deck, I couldn't move. Not even when a stray bullet whizzed past me and embedded into the mast a mere foot from me.

"Mistress!" Doc grabbed me by the waist and hauled me away. *"Are ye tryin' to get yerself killed?"*

• • •

Having recovered quickly, my shock turned to anger and something else I couldn't quite discern.

Angry that the captain lied to my face. He knew the other ship hadn't surrendered. There was no way an experienced captain like himself would miss something that the surgeon noticed in mere seconds.

Angry at his nonchalance when I was positively a wreck of nerves. Angry that he walked away from me not telling me that it very well could be the last time I saw him alive. I shuddered at the thought.

God, I would hate him forever if he died without saying goodbye.

That's when I realized what my other unsettling emotion was—worry. Worry for him, worry for us if he didn't return.

Was I crazy for feeling this way? The longer I waited for him to return, the more I thought about it, about him.

He was a strong and beloved leader, who treated his crew like family, saving them from a life of poverty and desolation. He took on Fish, a lost and frightened stowaway, and embraced him as part of that family.

He was brave and stoic. He saved me from God knows what kind of fate with the mutineers. He honored my claim to the wine, even though he could easily have refused, insisting it belong to the crew as an earned prize.

As a few of the men began to return, requiring medical attention, I realized that maybe my feelings for the captain weren't all that crazy.

Luckily, most of the men only had surface wounds and I could help Doc patch them up with only half my mind on the task.

The other half was thinking about all the things about the captain that I couldn't put into words.

How his touch paralyzed and lit me up at the same time. How just being in proximity to him felt like playing with fire. The heady feeling I got when his breath tickled my neck, the tension that built between my legs when his storm cloud eyes locked in on mine with a lustful hunger.

No, it wasn't crazy, it was real. And right now, as the metallic smell of blood drenched my senses in the surgery, I was stuck waiting to see if his touch would ever burn my skin and make my heart flutter again.

A groan grabbed my attention as a crew mate stumbled into the surgery with a small knife sticking out of his thigh.

"Come sit." I ushered him to one of the few sitting places in the surgery that wasn't already taken. He sat down, or more like fell, onto the crate, his injured leg straight out.

I recognized him, he was one of the twins. Either Jamie or Henry, I couldn't tell them apart.

I grabbed a fistful of bandages and kneeled down beside his skewered leg.

"Okay, I'm gonna have to pull this out. It will hurt like the devil, but once I staunch the bleeding, you'll be fine, alright? Now, give me your belt."

He nodded, his teeth chattering despite it being hot & muggy inside the surgery with all the extra bodies. I used his belt as a tourniquet, cinching it as tight as possible at the top of his thigh.

"On three... One... two." I ripped it out early and he howled. Another reason to be pissed off with the captain, he led the charge that landed this man with a knife in his leg. I wrapped his thigh tightly in linen and secured it with a pin.

"Up you go." I pulled him to his feet, hooking his arm over my shoulder, letting him displace his weight onto me. "I'll help you to your hammock and then stay there, you hear? I don't want you trying to run around being a hero and start the bleeding again. You'll be no help to anyone on this crew if you bleed to death."

"I don't think I'll have a hard time following your orders, my lady," he chuckled weakly.

• • •

Back in the surgery, every time the door opened, my heart skipped a beat and then fell when I realized it wasn't the captain.

That bastard, where was he?

As if on cue, I heard someone shout for him from outside the room. My ears pricked up and I stormed out the door

Oh, did I have things to say to the man.

When I saw him, it was an arresting juxtaposition to the first time I saw him. He was still covered in blood, sweat, and soot but whereas the first time I saw a monster, this time I saw a warrior. His knuckles were bruised and bloody. A spattering of blood layered on top of the black on his face and his bare chest glistened with sweat.

"Damn you, Elliot Cross!" I stormed to him and shoved his chest with both hands as hard as I could. When that barely moved him an inch, I took to pounding his chest with my fists.

"Damn you and all that talk about honor and surrender and argh!" I was fuming, I couldn't even finish my sentence. But just as mad as I was, I also felt tears threatening to break like a dam in relief seeing him alive and beautiful as ever.

"If you had gotten yourself killed, I swear to God I would have killed you myself." Just the thought made my throat tense up.

"That doesn't make any sense, my lady." He chuckled in spite of my furious rattling.

"*God,* I really hate you sometimes, you know that?" I threw my hands in the air and stalked away.

• • •

The sight of them seemed to hollow out my insides. A grave sense of loss permeated the air.

Three bodies lay like parcels, wrapped and sewn into a shroud made from their own hammock, two cannonballs at their feet. The crew stood in a semi-circle around them except for three men, one for each body.

The first man stepped forward and faced the crew. "Alexander James Morgan, beloved husband to Elizabeth and father to Beatrice, Marty and William." He tilted his head back as if he was trying to stop tears from spilling down his face. "Alex here was a real pain in the arse." The crew erupted in laughter. "But I don't think a pain in the arse will ever be missed so dearly."

The men had stopped laughing and nodded along solemnly. "He always fought bravely. Never left his men's backs unguarded, even if it meant his was."

Though I hadn't known the man well, my throat still closed up as I fought back tears. Father, husband, friend. The man knelt down beside his comrade and picked up the needle still threaded in the shroud. Alexander was already sewn up to his chin, his closed eyes and forehead revealed.

I felt like I was trespassing, an intruder of this intimate moment. I watched as the man hooked the needle through his friend's nose and I gasped. *He just stabbed the corpse!*

"To make certain, he's dead, ma'am." Jonas whispered next to me. The man made a cross over his deceased mate's shrouded face and returned to the crowd. His fellow crew mates clapped him on his back.

The sky was blue and hot, but it felt like the clouds hung heavy, feeling the weight of the burial. A weight that lay heavy on everyone, including the captain.

I spotted him a few people away. He stood tall, shoulders back. But not in the way of a proud, confident man standing erect. Rather a man who was accustomed to the position, despite the weight of the world bearing down on his shoulders. These were his men, their life and death in his hands.

The next man began speaking about the second shrouded man. I nuzzled my way through the crowd to be at the captain's side. He didn't look at me or acknowledge my presence at all, yet his tense body seemed to relax slightly. His balled fists unclenched.

I loosely took one of his hands in mine without a word, eyes straight ahead. He gave my hand a squeeze and my heart leaped. I may have been damn crazy for the way I felt about him, but he surely felt it too, clinging to me for support. I wanted to be that anchor for him. Absorb some of his pain, his tension.

My whole life I'd been told I needed a man but here was the bravest and strongest man I'd ever known, and he needed me.

A lone bagpipe began playing. The three bodies, having now been sewn shut, were lifted up on planks and balanced on the railing. The captain released my hand to stand in front of his men.

The captain's voice carried over the deck. "Unto Almighty God, we commend the souls of our brothers departed and we commit their bodies to the deep; in sure and certain hope of the resurrection unto eternal life, the sea shall give up her dead; and the corruptible bodies of those who sleep in her shall be changed. Amen."

The men holding the planks tipped one side up so the bodies of their comrades slid off and into the sea. Born of the earth, returned to the sea.

CHAPTER ELEVEN

Foolishness

I wasn't entirely sure whether it was a celebration for the prize taken or a wake for the men lost in the process, but Cook allowed for a few barrels of whiskey to be tapped and cooked a stew with two sources of meat instead of the strict one meat per meal rule.

When I first started helping with the rationing, Cook quickly set me straight when I brought both salted pork and beef to the galley. "Now, ye're just being wasteful," he'd grumbled. "Why would ye need both pig and cow? Ye wouldn't. So, stop this nonsense unless ye want to end up starving to death on this God forsaken ship."

So, when he had two chickens butchered and used some pork meat too, I knew it was an important night.

The usual rowdiness of the evening meal was amplified tenfold. And honestly, it was pleasant. After such a stressful morning and somber burial, watching the men forget they were pirates and drink and sing like they were normal men was cathartic.

"An olive branch..." I spun around to find the captain offering me a glass of whiskey. I accepted with a scowl.

"They really do surrender most of the time," he said.

"Mhmm, sure." The whiskey burned my sinuses as I took a sip. "So, what was different this time?"

"The passengers." He paused to sip, his eyes locked on me over the rim of his glass, and I nearly forgot what the hell we were talking about. I watched him swallow down the length of his long neck like a trail I wanted to travel. "Well, one passenger in particular. It was transporting the new governor of Santo Domingo. We'd been tipped off that he was traveling with enough coin to build himself a new governor's mansion and fortification for the island's entry points."

"I'm assuming they didn't want to give up such precious cargo so easily?"

"No, my lady. Nor did the captain want to appear weak to his new boss, aye."

"Men and their pride," I scoffed.

"Shall I fetch ye another, my lady?" I looked at him questioningly and he nodded to my glass which I hadn't even realized was empty already. *That was fast*. Looking around at the inebriated men stumbling all over each, I figured I could allow myself another too.

"Please." I handed him my glass. He sure seemed to be on his best behavior, trying to get back on my good side after my outburst this morning.

I was slightly embarrassed by my actions. It was scary showing how much I cared. It was like handing the man a sharpened arrow pointed right at my heart.

• • •

I collapsed onto a bench out of breath and my throat hoarse from belting song after song. One refill of whiskey turned into another and another. I was certain I was making a fool of myself but too drunk to care. Plus, I was having fun. And I'm sure half the men wouldn't remember tonight anyway.

"How'd I do?" I asked the captain sitting next to me. I had to almost shout over all the men still loudly bumbling about, despite the captain being less than a foot away.

"Voice of an angel, my lady." He gave me such a devilishly handsome grin, it made me want to wrap my hands around his neck and never let go. Having been relieved of my inhibitions thanks to the whiskey, just about anything the captain did made me want to climb into his lap.

He'd drank as well but clearly not as much as me. Which was evident when I nearly fell off the beach and his sharp reflexes caught me, his arm shooting out and catching me around the waist. His grip on me made my stomach flutter.

"I think it's time ye retire from the party, aye?" he said as he lifted me back to sitting upright.

"Aye, aye, Captain," I mocked him, and he shook his head with a turned-up smile.

Weaving through the crew's swaying hammocks, I think my inability to walk a straight line actually helped. The captain lit a lantern, and I noticed his shoulder was bleeding through his shirt.

"Captain." I swept up his hand and changed direction. "C'mon." I pulled him toward the surgery.

"Och, it's—"

"*Naught but a scratch*," I mimicked his low, gravelly voice while finishing his sentence. He reluctantly allowed me to drag him to the surgery.

I jumped up on the operation table and started barking drunken orders. "I'll need some fresh linen bandages from there." I pointed to the storage hutch across the room. "And some suture and needles from that drawer there."

"Woah, woah now lass, ye're not going anywhere near me with a needle in yer state."

"Oh shush." I swung my legs, having fun making him nervous.

"A few weeks on a pirate ship and ye think yerself a proper doctor now, do ye?"

"The supplies, Captain."

"Hey, aren't I the one who's supposed to be on the table and ye runnin' 'round."

"If you want me off the table, make me."

"No, no, I quite like the sight of ye on a table..." Humor dropped from his voice and chills ran down my back. He looked at me hungrily and teasingly, and I couldn't help but let a small smile crack on my face.

"Well, now that that's settled, get over here," I said, trying to shake off the lust that clung to me. Surely stabbing him with a needle would ruin the mood... I hoped, because the pounding in my core didn't seem to be going anywhere.

He stopped in front of me, setting the materials he gathered on the table. He stood at a respectful distance, about a foot in front of my knees, but it was too far to be able to properly stitch his cut and I told him as much. I parted my knees and pulled him closer, so he was standing in between them. His hands hovered over my thighs, as if debating whether or not to touch me, until finally deciding to put a hand on either thigh.

I tugged at his neckline, trying to reveal his wounded shoulder, but it was too far down his arm to see with his shirt on. I undid his top button, and he bit his lower lip. His breathing remained even and steady as I continued unbuttoning his shirt, mine however seemed to be catching with every breath. When I fumbled with the last button, he covered my hands with his and undid it before shrugging off the shirt completely.

I could hear the celebration still roaring down the hall and could still smell the blood on the surgery floor from this morning's wounded. Two contrasting results.

And in front of me stood the man responsible for all of it. The lantern light created shadows on his muscles, making them even more defined. A bruise bloomed on his ribs, and I lightly dragged my fingertips over it, desperate to touch him. I'd seen him—and most of the crew—shirtless more times than I could count, but for some reason his exposed skin now felt forbiddingly intimate. Like a test to see how far I'd really go.

He stood as still as a statue, a gorgeous Roman marble statue, and didn't flinch when I put pressure on his vivid purple bruise. "Any other injuries I should know about?"

He shook his head. "No, doctor," he nearly purred and my cheeks burned with heat.

"Good." I mentally kicked myself for getting distracted from the task at hand. *Would I ever be able to think straight when he was in front of me?*

I went to work cleaning and stitching the cut on his shoulder. He didn't say a word or move the entire time, except for when a hair fell into my face, and he brushed it behind my ear.

I finished wrapping his arm in bandages.

"Good as new," I said, proud of my work even in my drunken state. But he didn't move from his spot in between my knees, nor make a move to put back on his shirt.

I wrapped my arms around his neck slowly, almost to give him the chance to stop me. When he didn't, I did the thing I'd wanted to do for days. I pulled him closer and pressed my lips to his. Hesitantly at first, he grabbed my hips and crushed me to him with a low moan. My whole body flooded with heat and a matching moan escaped my lips.

His hands gripped my hips so hard I was certain I would have bruises tomorrow, but I didn't care. In fact, the idea of him leaving his mark on me only made my body throb more. All I cared about was his soft lips crushing against mine and his tongue searching mine out with a hungry need. His hands left my hips and roamed my body, lighting little fires everywhere he touched. I tangled my fingers in his hair, feeling like I couldn't get close enough to him. He tugged on my bottom lip with his teeth, and I let out a breathy sound. Seemingly encouraged by this, he shifted to kissing and nipping a trail down my neck. I threw my head back offering it all to him.

I was hot and light-headed, digging my fingernails into his shoulder when he returned to hungrily kissing my lips, like he'd gone weeks without food and I was a whole damn feast.

His masculine scent only heightened the experience: it was intoxicating, making me wonder how much was the whiskey and how much was him.

But when he started to slide his hands up my legs under my dress, I shivered. His callused hands were pleasantly rough along my skin. *Yes. Please.* I wanted this, wanted him so much. I drank in his kisses.

His gliding hands crept higher until he suddenly pulled away and jumped back like he'd touched a flame.

"I'm sorry, my lady, I shouldna treat ye in such a way."

"I want this, Captain." I tried to take his hand and pull him to me again, but he dodged me. Hot tears stung in my eyes, and I suddenly felt so exposed and insecure despite being the only one fully dressed.

"Ye should get to bed." My eyes lit up for a moment. "Alone," he clarified.

I jumped off the table and stared at him hurt and confused.

"I'll walk ye back now."

"Don't bother," I shot back before tears could choke my words. Was I really going to let this bloody pirate make me cry? It must have been the alcohol making me emotional, I tried to tell myself, even though I knew it was a damned lie.

I locked the cabin door and collapsed onto the hanging bed. Through a cracked window, I could hear waves crash against the ship in an unstoppable battering.

I was the ship and all the emotions and sensations that the captain stirred in me were the waves. I could no more stop the way I felt for the captain than the ship could stop the waves.

• • •

The next morning, I didn't want to get out of bed. Not only because of the previous night's humiliating incident but also because my head felt like it was filled with little gnomes trying to pickax their way out.

Fish's soft voice called for me from behind the door and I pulled the quilt over my head, trying to burrow away from my problems.

The captain's abrupt switch last night left an unsatisfied desire inside me like smoldering coals fighting to reignite.

With a groan, I threw the covers off and eventually got out of bed. Fish was still waiting outside my door, and he was the only person below deck that didn't look painfully hungover. Whiskey and ale still hung in the air, threatening to make whatever remained in my stomach come back up.

Fresh air. I needed it. And possibly needed to throw myself overboard too.

I was not looking forward to seeing the captain and wondered how long I could avoid him.

"Mistress, you alright?" I looked down at Fish and

realized I'd been standing, unmoving, at the base of the steps.

"Just dandy," I groaned and mounted the first step.

• • •

There were only two more days on board before we reached land and, in that time, I'd become exceptionally adept at pretending the captain was invisible. I knew I was being petty, but my ego was still so bruised by his rejection.

He would ask me a question and I'd give him one-word answers. He'd save me a seat at his table for dinner and I'd choose a table across the room.

Even Fish noticed we'd stopped taking our habitual walks.

On the last day, the captain came into my cabin, *his* cabin, to get the ledger and I barely acknowledged his presence.

"Ye can't ignore me forever."

"I can try," I said, my eyes remaining squarely on the book I was reading.

"Aye." He came to stand over my place on the bed. "You can try." His voice had an edge to it like he was getting sick of waiting for me to crack. He undid his top button and tugged on his neckline

He wanted to taunt me? *Fine, two can play that game.*

I sat up so I was kneeling on the bed and eye level with him. I wrapped one hand around his head and pulled him close. My lips were so close they were almost grazing his ear, I heard his breath hitch.

"There's a lot of things people have told me I couldn't do," I whispered in his ear. "And I proved them wrong every single time."

CHAPTER TWELVE

Land Hoes

"Ah, my sweet Cherry—She'll keep me bed real warm tonight." The men howled with laughter in response and made more crude insinuations about the women waiting for them on shore.

We had anchored off the coast of Nassau and I was currently packed on a rowboat to shore with six other crew members. The water was so clear that I could see colorful fish swimming just below the surface. The white sand ahead was dotted with tents and makeshift structures, but was still inviting, nonetheless. My legs itched to get foot on solid land.

Palm trees swayed in the wind and the shouts of hawkers grew louder the closer we got to the dock. Half of me was disgusted by the way the men only talked about their women like playthings, but the other half of me was envious that they had people waiting for them. I was still a stranger in a strange land and just as far away from New Bern as ever.

The small boat was pulled into dock and no sooner was it tied than the men jumped out and took off running. *Men.* I rolled my eyes.

The captain, Fish and Jonas were on a rowboat right behind us and I waited on the dock. I didn't want to wait for them, but I also had no idea where to stay or where to go.

They docked and the captain raised his eyebrows at me with a side smile. *God, why did he have to be so damn handsome.*

One would think that after what he did, it would ruin any appeal. But in fact, it was the opposite. Feeling his lips on mine only made them more attractive. Digging my nails into his back only made his sculpted body more breathtaking. And after his hands explored places they hadn't been before, it was all I could think about. *What would happen if he hadn't stopped?*

"Waiting for us, are ye?" *God, I hated him.*

"I wouldn't if I didn't have to," I said. "We need to make arrangements for my wine." He nodded and kept walking to the beach.

"You in a hurry to get somewhere?" I followed him while Jonas and Fish unloaded the boat. "The *whore house* perhaps? Like the rest of your men," I hissed.

He spun around so quickly, I walked straight into him. He steadied me with a firm grip on my arms. His hands locked me in place in front of him. But not in an embrace, more like a vice. My body hummed being this close to him again and I had to try my damnedest to glare at him and not kiss him. *What was wrong with me?*

"No, I'm no goin' to the *whore house.*" His voice was low and deep, deep like his

eyes that froze me to the spot. "There's only one woman for me." My stomach dropped.

He had a woman waiting for him in Nassau.

He leaned down to whisper in my ear, the same way I teased him yesterday in his cabin. "And I'll be havin' her very soon." It was a possessive growl that made the hairs on the back of my neck stand up.

His mouth so close to where he had kissed my neck just nights ago gave me a chill. I shook myself from his grip. The wine could wait. I wouldn't stand here and be disrespected like this. Furious at myself for expecting anything different from a goddamn pirate.

"I'm finding a room. We'll settle with the wine tomorrow," I said over my shoulder.

I stalked away not knowing where I was going, but not caring as long as it was away from him.

• • •

The town of Nassau was far different from anywhere I'd been before. People in the colonies always dressed modestly, no matter how hot it was. Men in trousers, women in long sleeve dresses. It wasn't just out of modesty, it's what was acceptable for the public.

But here, men and boys ran around in pants torn just above the knee. Women wore bright colored dresses that hung loosely from their bodies and barely covered their shoulders. Less than half were even wearing a stay and some women's dresses were simply fabric wrapped around them, a big slit where the fabric hung open.

And the people themselves were in every shade from the darkest ebony to sunburnt gingers with innumerable freckles.

People sold art and textiles in the streets and exotic fruit I'd never seen before. The wind carried with it fresh sea breeze, unlike the harsh fish smell of Beaufort. Buildings seemed to be stuck between reconstruction and crumbling apart—it appeared people just added new stories, porches and wings to buildings without fixing previous degradation, making it look like a mix matched quilt stitched together in a chaotic indistinguishable pattern.

Unlike New Bern, which was carefully constructed in a grid to create organized roads and blocks, the streets of Nassau wriggled like a snake in between the crooked buildings and shacks made of raw materials like hides, driftwood and dried reeds.

After asking a passerby for directions, I found an eclectic boarding house and booked myself a room. I didn't have any money on me, but when I mentioned I came in with Captain Cross, the innkeeper insisted it would be free of charge. *Interesting.*

He was a jolly man with bushels of unruly gray hair and a matching beard twisted into a braid. His welcoming hospitality made me think of Margaret and my heart sank.

I still couldn't believe she betrayed me in such a horrible way. If it wasn't for her, I never would be on some Caribbean island pining after a damn pirate captain.

And speaking of the captain, how could I have not realized he had a woman waiting for him on land?

I certainly wouldn't put it past a pirate to be unfaithful—which made me his concubine. I hated the thought. No wonder he didn't take things further in the surgery, his conscious must have finally kicked in. It made me feel so dirty.

"Here we are, Mistress, if ye need anything else just holler." The innkeep held the room's door open for me and handed me the key.

"Thank you, sir. Actually, some parchment and ink would be very helpful, if it's not too much trouble."

"No trouble at all, my lady, any friend of the captain's is a friend of mine." I wondered if he'd still think so highly of the captain if he knew he was a filthy, cheating bastard.

The innkeep left with a smile, whistling a song I recognized from the pirate ship as he walked away.

The room was small but much nicer than I expected. I had expected a simple pallet and a blanket but instead, there was a full-size bed, a second-story balcony and a vanity with a wash basin.

I was admiring the view of the beach from the balcony, when the innkeep returned minutes later with my requests. Using the banister as a table, I began to write my letter. It had been weeks and my poor parents still had no idea what happened to me. They certainly deserved to know that I was at least alive.

I kept my letter brief and to the point. They didn't need to hear details about having pirates as bunkmates and my frustrating infatuation with a particular pirate captain. All they needed to know was that I was alive, unharmed—at least physically—and would be returning to Beaufort with the wine in a week's time, give or take.

I signed the letter with a sigh, feeling some relief knowing that my parents would finally be reassured. I came back inside and set it on the vanity to take with me the next time I left the inn.

I looked at myself in the vanity mirror—the first time I'd seen my reflection in weeks.

My honey blonde hair was streaked with lighter, sun-bleached strips. My face and chest were a rosy olive, having tanned substantially from being in the sun so much. My cheekbones were more pronounced, and I was shocked by how much thinner I looked.

The humid sea air had turned every piece of hair that wasn't pinned or tied up in a plait into curly coils creating a halo of frizz.

Looking at myself, I tried to imagine what the captain's woman—*wife?*—looked like. She was undoubtedly beautiful. They probably looked like a work of art together. Picturing them together made me sick.

I racked my mind for an explanation on how I could be so stupid.

There was a knock at my door. Assuming it was Fish or the innkeep, I told them to come in. The door slowly opened, and I watched in the reflection as the captain walked in. Anger and frustration flooded my cheeks with warmth.

"If you've come to explain your island lover, I don't want to hear it." I didn't turn around, just glowered at him through the mirror.

"Is that what ye think?" The low timber of his voice was like a vibration straight to my core. "That the woman, *my* woman, is some mistress of Nassau?"

"Yes, and quite frankly, I don't know why you're here and not somewhere with her. Surely, she's expecting you to come running into her bed."

He laughed, and rage and hurt boiled inside me. He came closer and I refused to turn around and face him.

"For such an intelligent woman, ye can be real daft, ye know that?" He was now so close his breath was like a feathery touch on my neck. I couldn't believe how his close proximity made my knees weak, even when he was insulting me. I wanted him more than anything, but I also hated him so much in that moment.

"Did you come here just to insult me?" I struggled to not let my tumultuous feelings leak into my voice.

"It's you, Sloane." With a firm hand on my hip, he spun me around. "It's *only* you." He pushed up against the vanity and clasped my face in his other hand, forcing me to look up at him. My breaths became ragged and uneven as I felt his desire for me grow in his pants, pressing against my stomach.

It was me. I was his woman.

The realization made my pulse flutter and sweet tension coil in the pit of my stomach. I bit my lip as I stared back into his icy gray eyes. The desire I saw staring back at me made a puddle between my legs.

He gently twirled a strand of my hair. "I want ye so bad it pains me." His gentle twirling turned into a clenched fist.

"I need to call ye mine," he groaned, and his fist trembled with what seemed like the effort to control himself.

But I didn't want him to contain himself. I wanted him to lose control. I wanted to feel the unleashed power of Captain Elliot Cross.

"Then do it," I dared him. "Make me yours."

Like uncaging a wild beast, he growled and crushed his mouth against mine. And I opened for him, letting his kisses consume me with their passion. He hoisted me up, so I was sitting on the vanity, my back flat against the mirror.

With a frenzied hunger, I clawed at his shirt, desperate to feel his hot skin under my hands, to rake his back with my nails.

At the same time, he rustled up the layers of my skirt, his hands finishing the journey they'd started nights ago.

Heat rushed to my groin, and I gasped when his fingers brushed against my sensitive lips. He continued to slide his fingers in delicious circles around the apex of my thighs and I buried my face into his neck, the sensations so dizzying I couldn't focus on even kissing straight.

I mewled at his touch, bucking into his hands and he moaned, a sound that made me all the more desperate to have him, *all of him.*

I fumbled with his belt, the fabric of his breeches strained over his bulge. I had

never done this before, but it didn't matter. My body knew what it wanted, *needed*, and ancient animal instincts took over.

His length sprang free, and he shoved my knees apart

before fisting my hair and tugging my head back, so his eyes were locked on mine.

"Once I start, I willna be able to stop," he growled, part warning, part promise and I answered him by wrapping my legs around his waist and crushing him to me.

It felt like every inch of my body was a spark of lightning, waiting for him to make his claim to it.

He thrust into me, so deep and hard I let out a sound I didn't even recognize as myself. Covering my mouth with his, he slid partially out before pounding in again. A moan passed from between his lips into mine, and I couldn't help but lift my hips to meet his next thrust. I'd always heard the first time was supposed to hurt, but *God, it felt so good.*

Just as I was getting used to the fullness of having him inside me, he dropped his hand back to that sweet spot he'd been teasing before. The sensations were overwhelming in the most amazing way. I dug my fingers into his bare buttocks trying to stay grounded in the moment, in reality, as his primal loving was taking me higher and higher.

The tension between my thighs and wrapping around his cock was becoming almost unbearable. "Captain...oh God... what is... I can't..." My legs began to quiver, and I was sure I was going to burst.

"It's alright, just let go." His husky whisper was what finally took me over the edge. I let go. Surrendered to every buzzing, delicious sensation inside me and it was more than alright. It was bloody unbelievable.

I was panting and still shattering into pieces as he continued his relentless massage of the sweet nub between my legs. And then he hit his moment too. Taking one final plunge into me, his deepest and hardest yet, his back stiffened and arched, as he groaned my name.

I traced my fingers down his cheek, bringing his face to mine. "Elliot..." I whispered into his lips and in his arms.

"*My* lady," he answered.

CHAPTER THIRTEEN

On the Island

The next two days were a blur of commotion. The captain got called away shortly after we finished on the vanity. Since then, we'd barely had a minute alone, surviving off stolen kisses in corridors and knowing looks from across the room.

We decided that the captain and his men would sail back to the colonies to deliver my wine. It was too risky sending it back with another merchant and risk getting it stolen again. For the rest of the goods, the captain made introductions to the island's most reputable fences, and I took over negotiations.

They all underestimated me when we first met. But by the time we reached a deal, there wasn't a single one that didn't respect me. One man even offered me a job. A flattering offer, but I was itching to get back home. The captain assured me the men were working as fast as possible to get the ship stocked and ready for departure.

Once there was nothing left for me to sell, the captain suggested another way for me to pass the time. I'd been reading on the beach when he approached me, leading two horses. They were both obsidian black and shone in the bright sun. "I have something I want to show ye," he said, handing me the reins to one horse and jumping on the other.

We rode for hours judging by the sun's falling position in the sky. Granted, half the time I couldn't even see the sun through the dense tree canopy. We climbed through the jungle, the horses intuitively following a seemingly invisible trail. The vibrant and varied greens that cloaked our surroundings were awe inspiring.

I'd never been anywhere so untouched by humans but still so humming with life. Innumerable birds filled the air with their songs and calls to one another. I knew the backcountry of the colonies could be wild and untamed, but when I traveled with my father, we never strayed from the known travel routes, visiting already cleared homesteads.

This was peerless. Centuries of growth spilled over each other in tumbling vines, blossoming foliage and towering ancient trees.

As I watched the captain lead the way, I fluctuated between giddy nervousness and calm. Our first time was so unexpected, I hadn't had time to be nervous. It happened so fast, and I was so swept up in all the sensations—it was like my body overrode my mind.

My body ached to be close to him like that again. Each time I thought of it, a crash of butterflies would hit, and my skin would tingle, eager for his touch. But having time to actually think about it, nerves and insecurities would flood my mind.

The way he made my body sing, I knew I couldn't be his first, far from it.

That didn't bother me, I figured at least one of us should know what we're doing. But I couldn't help equating my inexperience with my inevitable lack of skill.

And then there was the calm. That was perhaps the dominate feeling. Being with him was like the comforting, mindless lulling of a rocking chair. Steady, present, supporting.

And there was no question in my mind about his feelings for me. It was there in the chill of his eyes, a heat mingled with the cool gray. I felt it in the way he lost himself inside me, like a missing piece finally falling into place. The way he had to actively constrain himself so his desire wouldn't consume me.

The setting sun broke through the leaves in rays of gold, highlighting the small but discernible pink scratches I'd left on his back. That made me smile.

"Hey mister!" I wasn't far behind him but had to shout to be heard over the cacophony of jungle noises. "Where are you taking me?"

He only grinned over his shoulder and shrugged, *the bastard.* "Well, can you at least tell me if we're close? My arse is killing me." I heard his rumbling laugh.

"I'll kiss it better." His promise carried back to me and my cheeks instantly burned. *Was that ever going to stop? Or would I just need to accept the fact that I'd live the rest of my life looking like an embarrassed strawberry?*

At last, he halted his horse at the top of the slope we'd been climbing for the last hour. I rode up alongside him and gasped.

It was a vision painted by God himself.

The sky was the most gorgeous mix of cherry blossom pink, dusky orange and lavender. Painted with expert strokes, it seemed to bloom from the horizon. It reflected over the ocean, which we looked down on, creating a rippling mirror image.

The thick forest we'd been surrounded by thinned drastically on the ocean-facing slope. Still lush, but instead of tall sprawling trees with trunks as thick as a house, this side was dotted with low bushes and skinny saplings fighting to take root against the coastal breeze

"Captain..." I managed to squeak out, "I'm speechless." *Speechless*, that word recalled Lord Thomas' smarmy face as he presented that gaudy necklace. This view trumped any necklace money could ever buy. This was true beauty. And I was blessed to be sharing it with my pirate captain instead of a stuffy lord.

I reached between the horses to hold his hand. "Thank you," I whispered, my throat suddenly tight with emotion.

"The rest is on foot, hobble yer horse up here." The downhill was steep but manageable, and I trailed behind him, holding onto bushes for support.

A roofline became visible about halfway down and I realized that was our destination.

It was a small, single platform structure jutting out from the cliffside, the roof covering it at an angle. The captain climbed a ladder made of branches tied together with crude rope. I wondered how he was going to get in, since the whole platform was encased in a wall made of reeds like a box. But when he reached the top, he simply undid some sort of latch and then began to roll the wall back.

It wasn't a solid wall at all, but rather a screen that could fully roll up creating a deck that was open on all sides.

"Your turn," he called down to me, and I started to climb the ladder. He offered his hand to me at the top and in the same motion, he pulled me to his chest, wrapping his arms tightly around my waist and crushing his lips against mine.

I responded by melting into him and tangling my fingers in his hair to draw him even closer to me. He planted feather-light kisses from my clavicle up my neck to that tender spot just behind my ear and warmth flooded my core. When he bit my earlobe and gently sucked it into his mouth, I let out a breathy moan.

"If ye keep making little noises like that, we'll never make it to the beach," he groaned.

"The beach?" He gave the other side of my neck the same treatment, eliciting another soft moan.

"Ye drive me wild, my lady," he said breathlessly. *Me?* Driving this ungodly handsome man wild? He'd seen me at my lowest, dirty and battered, and still he chose me. And my better judgment be damned, I chose him too.

He nestled his face into my shoulder. "Come, lass, and stop distracting me, I had a plan," he groaned into my chest before placing one last kiss on my bosom and stepping back.

"A plan to kiss me like your life depended on it and then stop? *Some plan*," I scoffed and put my hands on my hips to glare at him crossly. "And all before you even get me undressed." I shook my head and pulled out the pins securing my gown to my stomacher and shrugged the gown off, letting it pool in a heap behind me. He grabbed my hands and plastered them to my side before I could start unpinning the stomacher from my stay.

"Ye can never make anything easy, can ye?" He laughed, bending over a trunk I hadn't noticed before he swept me up in our kiss. He took out a roll of linens and nodded to the ladder. "Down ye go."

"Are you not going to lead the way?" I had no idea what he was up to, but it was fun not knowing.

He came up behind me. "I'm no' turnin' my back on ye, ye vixen..." he drawled before slapping my arse.

I yelped but couldn't help flushing at the hot impact. I shot him a look over my shoulder before starting down the ladder. "I'll get you back for that," I promised.

"I canna wait."

The beach at the bottom wasn't like the cluttered beach in Nassau that seemed to house half the population in tents and lean-tos. It felt like we were the first people to touch this beach. Pristine didn't even cover it.

The turquoise water lazily lapped at the pearly white sand. The sunset left everything in a dreamy haze.

I startled when arms wrapped around my waist and a nose nuzzled the back of my neck sending chills down my arms. The captain held the linen towel in front of me, resting on top was a soap bar blended with colorful flowers slightly muted by the soap covering them. I picked up the bar and inhaled the delicate scent. I caught whiffs of gardenia and jasmine and something else I didn't recognize.

"I know ye didna plan on spending weeks on a grimy pirate ship. Thought I could try to rectify that." I leaned back into him, trying to remember what it felt like to be clean.

"You're just trying to get me naked." I spun around to face him, still clutched in his arms.

"Oh, most definitely, my lady." He lowered his head so our mouths were nearly touching, "And I thought I would help with the soapin' too." He closed the distance between our lips, and I struggled to wrap my mind around where I was and who I was with.

It felt like I'd been catapulted into someone else's life these past weeks. And with the captain's lips molding with mine, I was jealous and grateful for the woman's life I'd stepped into. A part of me cherished this new connection with the confidence that it may be new, but it won't be short-lived.

But another, nagging part of me kept whispering this wouldn't last, that the captain would never truly be mine.

"Turn around, lass." I'd been so caught up in my own head and his kisses—they seemed to do that a lot—that I hadn't noticed he'd unpinned my stomacher and it now lay in the sand.

I turned and felt the gentle tug as he untied my petticoats until they pooled in a ring around me and I was left standing in just my stockings, shift and stay.

He came back around to my front, taking my hand as I stepped out of the pile of garments. He lowered to a kneel, never breaking eye contact. His eyes stormed with lust, and I felt my breath catching, especially when he placed one of my feet on his knee and teasingly slow, dragged his hands up my thigh.

With the same sensual care, he untied my stocking, rolled it down and off. So much had changed since the first time he removed my stockings like this.

He stalked behind me before brushing my hair over my shoulder to access the laces of the stay. I felt each loop being undone, the fire growing steadily in my belly with each one.

Coming back in front of me, he slid the stay down my arms and tossed it to join the rest of my clothes, mere barriers to him being able to have all of me.

My shift was sheer, and like a typical man, his eyes immediately dropped to my breasts, their rosy buds just visible through the thin material. I bit my lip, and I could have sworn an almost silent moan came from the captain.

"Fair is fair." I stopped his hands from pulling my shift off and instead started undressing him.

With a little help from me, he stepped out of his breeches. His long shirt hung to mid-thigh, leaving most of him still covered. I steadied myself before reaching for the hem. I'd never seen a man in the nude before, let alone one I was undeniably attracted to. I hadn't even seen those parts of him the first time he took me. *I'd been kidnapped twice and survived, how scary could this be?*

I gathered the hem in my hands as I raised it. As if in sync with the shirt, he grew harder and higher. I swallowed at the sight. *That fit inside me?*

He lifted his arms so I could pull his shirt completely off.

God he was beautiful. All of him.

I dragged my fingers along the now almost healed cut I'd stitched up. It was far from his only scar. Like a tapestry of his combat stories, his entire body was carved with souvenirs.

Scars I'd never noticed before decorated his chest and I couldn't help pressing my lips to them, feeling him jerk slightly. Did he not like me touching them? Or was he simply trying to restrain himself while I kissed his naked body?

My bet was the latter.

I stood up with a smirk and saw his eyes were pressed tightly closed in focus. *Definitely the latter.*

"Finish your job, Captain," I said, feeling increasingly confident after seeing his reaction to my touch.

I rolled my shoulders back and tilted my head to the side, accentuating the curve of my bare neck.

With one hand, he slowly undid the bow closing the neck of the flimsy linen. He hooked a finger under the neckline of my shift, pulling it down my shoulder before doing the same to the other. He paused for a moment when the shift dropped, leaving me fully exposed. His eyes darkened with desire.

Then like kindling catching fire, igniting into flames in seconds, the slow and teasing pace was gone, and he crushed our bodies together, his mouth hungrily devouring mine.

The feel of his bare body on mine was an inexplicable feeling of coming home, becoming a whole when I never even knew I was missing pieces.

His hands cupped my buttocks and I jumped into him, wrapping my legs around his waist, arms tightly around his neck. My tongue explored his mouth as he carried me toward the water. We fell into the ocean, still locked in our embrace.

The motion of the tide moved me up and down on his lap, causing my heat to slide along his shaft. The sensation of him between my lips and the promise of what was to come made my heart drop in my chest, like when your foot slips on a step and abruptly catches you on the next one.

His hands roamed my back and hair as he groaned into our kisses. Emboldened, I reached in between us and guided him into my entrance. He filled me with a wave of sensations that made me toss my head back moaning his name.

Like we'd done this a thousand times, he began licking and nipping my neck without missing a beat. He simultaneously lifted me up by my hips before pounding me back down while he thrusted up. Hitting a spot that sent stars to my eyes, I arched my back as he clutched me to his chest.

"Ye're so damn beautiful," he breathed into my mouth as he covered mine in his and continued pumping into me. With our position and how tightly we were pressed together, my most sensitive nub rubbed up against him until I was panting, that delicious pressure building.

I could tell from his strained breathing that he was close too. I squeezed my eyes shut and bit down on his lip as I tried to hold off tumbling from the edge.

"I have to let go," I mewled and with one last glide across his body, I burst with pleasure, a tingling release spread to all my limbs. I cried out, unable to hold in the overwhelming sensations.

"Oh Sloane, making ye scream drives me—" He let loose an equally enjoyed groan and shuddered then stilled inside me.

The water was close to bath water, so different from the frigid Atlantic that lined the coast of the colonies. I floated dreamily on my back as the captain fetched the soap from the beach. The slow, undulating rock of the warm water surrounding me was like the physical manifestation of post-lovemaking bliss.

The sky was now a dark lavender, the first stars just becoming visible. The moon was full and bright making the water silvery in its light.

Captain stayed true to his word and glided across my body with soap. His hands like the serpent in the Garden of Eden, slithering on my skin with tempting pleasure.

He worked the soap into a lather and patiently combed the tangles out of my hair with his fingers. Only interrupting his tasks for kisses that were small and light but still left me feeling light-headed and clenching my thighs.

Returning the favor, I was able to caress his body with real attention for the first time. Dragging my palm down his torso, I could feel each etched muscle, each ragged scar. I ran my hands down his arms and felt a chill ripple under my touch despite the tepid water.

I couldn't get over the haughty feeling I got each time this fierce and fearsome pirate captain squirmed in response to my touch. I circled my hands around him to catch his cheeks. I squeezed his buttocks and laughed when he jumped in response.

"What are ye up to, lass?" He smirked, acting like he didn't like it, though the growing hardness between us begged to differ.

"You have a nice, plump arse," I giggled and gave it another squeeze.

"Aye, mayhap." He reached around my waist to grip my behind. "But 'tis no' as fine as yers." He tightened his hold on my cheeks so much I yelped and released his.

He twirled me in the water, one arm like a bar across my chest, the other cinched around my waist. "As the captain, I am the one in charge here," he purred into my ear and my heart rate spiked. "And I have a mind to remind ye of that."

He tightened his arms, effectively locking me against him. The wind danced across my shoulders exposed above the water giving me a chill, but the captain's body burned like an inferno against my back.

"We're nowhere near the ship, Captain." I squirmed, testing his restraint and a small thrill ran through me when I discovered there was no way I was escaping his grasp.

"Aye, but a ship doesna make the captain." His hand around my waist slipped down my thigh, and I couldn't help but gasp when he slid it back up to cup between my legs. He dragged two fingers through my folds. "And this is for all the times ye mouthed off, refused my orders, even struck me, and made me want ye so bad it nearly burned me up." He thrust two fingers inside me, and my body clenched around him.

"I knew ye'd be mine, Sloane, from the moment I met ye, ye stubborn fool refusing to take my hand." He continued to pump the fingers inside me and worked his thumb on the outside. "Though, I'd be lyin' if I wasna a wee bit disappointed when I couldna throw ye o'er my shoulder."

He was right, I'd always been his. He was my calm and my anchor among the chaos and carnage of that day. Even covered in the blood of other men, I went with him. I clung to his hand as if the ocean would reach up and swallow me whole if I let go.

His hand continued to wind the need that was tighten-

157

ing within me. I rocked back against him, my breaths coming in raggedy moans. He slowed to an excruciating pace.

"Captain," I begged, "please."

"Ye'll have yer pleasure when I decide to give it." He bit my shoulder and I groaned.

"God, please." The tension was so intense now, but his feather-light pressure did nothing to alleviate it. I couldn't believe I was begging.

"God can no' help ye now, lass," His voice was deep, dark, and husky, making me bloom with warmth.

"I swear if you don't—" A sharp and deep thrust of his fingers inside me took my words. He chuckled in my ear, his pace now relentless.

"Oh God," I cried out as the tension burst, ecstasy coursing through my body until I was limp, his arms now keeping me from going below the surface.

He pressed his lips to my neck and whispered something so faint I couldn't make it out.

• • •

"Why did you stop..." I trailed a finger down his chest, my head rested in the crook of his shoulder. We lay on a bed of sheepskin in the tree house, a fine sea breeze cooling us after yet another passionate session of loving. "That night in the surgery, after the prize ship?"

"Aye, ye were none too pleased with that." Our bodies, pressed together, were slightly sticky with sweat and island humidity. A feeling that would be gross if shared with anyone else, but with him it just felt raw and right.

"Ye were more than a wee bit into the drink. I didna want yer first time to be one ye might not remember. Didna feel right to have ye like that."

"So, you did want me?" I couldn't believe how insecure my voice sounded, I didn't think that even now, his rejection from that night would still sting.

"O'course I wanted ye." He whipped around so I was now flat on my back, and he hovered over me. "I wanted ye the first night I tended to yer wounds." He pressed a kiss to my lips, then growled, "And would ha'e killed the bastards that hurt ye if I hadn't already done so." He kissed me hard, almost aggressive, as if remembering the anger he'd felt.

"I wanted ye when ye were all cute and flustered after ye thought I was makin' ye my whore—"

"Hey, I wasn't acting cute, I was furious at you!"

"I wanted to prove yer assumption correct and take ye right then." He stifled my protest with another kiss before dipping his head to run his tongue up my neck.

"I wanted ye on every walk we took 'round the deck..." Kisses were planted in a line in between my breasts as his head bobbed lower. "Had to fight the urge to bend ye over the railing and make ye scream every damn day." That increasingly familiar heat between my legs pulsed. *Maybe we could still make that sizzling mental image a reality.*

"And when ye took my blade to McDonald's throat, lass, I thought I was gonna die wanting ye so bad." *A man who wasn't threatened by my strength and boldness, but admired it?* I thought I might die wanting *him*.

I reached for his face, but he pinned my arms at my side and bit my stomach in reprimand.

"And now yer gonna lay here and let me make up for all those times." He kissed a trail from my belly button to the crease of my hip, making me squirm with desire.

His eyes were locked on mine and the moonlight made his storm-colored eyes heavier, or maybe it was just my lust for the man projecting. With each kiss, his eyes closed briefly, as if he were savoring my taste.

His kisses drew closer to my womanhood and nerves ran through me. "Are you gonna kiss me...there?" My voice came out timid and reserved. *Would he really do that?*

"Aye, and I plan to do a lot more than just kissin'," My cheeks flushed like mad, as if my body had forgotten I'd spent the whole day naked and intimate with the man. "Would ye like that, my lady?"

The flutter in my stomach grew stronger and all I could do was nod. I'm pretty sure I'd like his mouth anywhere on my body. He gave me a devilish grin, then hooked one of my legs over each of his shoulders and dipped between my thighs.

The first contact of his tongue dragging through my lips sent a shock wave through my body. I felt him laugh at my reaction before sucking the most sensitive part into his mouth. I gasped, simply overwhelmed.

It was completely different from the feel of his fingers. And I loved it.

He sucked and circled that spot with his tongue, flicking that little pearl side to side, up and down. His mouth was warm and wet on my heat, and I moaned his name.

He took me by surprise when he drove two fingers into my wetness, and I released a groan he matched hungrily.

Hearing him enjoy pleasuring me had me bucking into his mouth. I twisted my fingers into the sheepskin beneath me as the tension grew to a climax.

With fast and sudden movement, he flipped me on to my stomach, yanked my hips into the air and thrust into me before I'd even finished spiraling. He filled me in a new position that seemed to hit undiscovered epicenters of pleasure that kept the waves racking through my body.

I only had a chance to catch my breath and calm my shaking body once he finished and collapsed onto me. The smell of sweat from exertion carried down to me, it was an inexplicably intoxicating scent, and I drank it in. His arms circled me, and he rolled us both onto our sides.

And that's how I fell asleep, cradled in his arms in a heady haze of bliss.

CHAPTER FOURTEEN

The Return Journey

I woke to find the spot next to me empty. The captain was already awake and probably on deck. We were arriving in Beaufort today, weather permitting. It was really a very easy journey when you're not being kidnapped by mutineers, raided by pirates or hunting Spanish prize ships.

I took my time getting ready, knowing that if anyone needed me, Fish would come knocking. I hoped he would stay with us in the colonies. I realized I hadn't actually broached the subject with Elliot yet, just assumed.

He and I had discussed what was next for him and the crew. I knew none of the men wanted to be pirates for life, they just didn't have any better opportunities. Elliot was a skilled captain, and his crew were strong sailors. I knew the Sinclair Trading Company could benefit from not only having a ship and crew in our employ to help expand our import business—especially now that the wine had been repossessed—but one that knew how to fight and survive on the sea. *I'd love to see anyone try to board my captain's ship.*

I purchased some new garments in Nassau before we set sail, a front-lacing stay for one, so that I could actually dress and undress myself. My current gown was a pale yellow that reminded me of the sunrise we woke up to in the tree house. Whenever I thought about that day and all the different cords Elliot strummed that I didn't even know were within me...well let's just say I don't think it crossed my mind once without pink flooding my cheeks and something else flooding between my legs.

The only thing that felt weird about the whole situation was how not weird it felt. Being with him was both effortless and joyful. He was attracted to me as a woman but respected me as a person. I wasn't smart for a woman, I was just smart. I wasn't brave for a woman, I was just brave. I wasn't good at business for a woman, I was just good at business.

Whenever I got nervous about introducing him to my father, I reminded myself of that. He may be a pirate, but he's also my rescuer. As much as I'd like to think I would have crafted my way out of my situation with the mutineers, my prospects were looking pretty slim at the time. He also broke McDonald's nose for laying a hand on me, something my father would surely agree with.

Yes, he was a pirate, but he wasn't the pirate who stole our wine and nearly killed Malcolm and he certainly wasn't responsible for the attack that killed my father's twin.

When I added it all up in my head, there was no way my father wouldn't approve. I'd sent him a letter our first day in Nassau, assuring him of my wellbeing and when I expected to be arriving back in Beaufort with the wine. At the time I was still mad at Elliot and made no mention of him continuing to be a part of my life once back in the colonies. I hoped my mother at least would be pleased I'd found a man that I would be happy to marry.

That thought made me freeze, my fingers stuck in a half-woven plait in my hair. *Marriage?*

Would I really be ready and willing to marry Captain Elliot Cross? Sure, the notion had crossed my mind in passing moments, but never had I so confidently stated my willingness, even if only in my own head.

I didn't have to drown in my thoughts for much longer; a knock came at my door drawing my attention. I hastily finished my plait, pinned it up and opened the door.

"Jonas?" I was surprised to see the bulking man. I'd figured all hands would be on deck to get us to shore in time.

"G'day Mistress, Cap'n wanted to let ye know that winds are stronger than expected but Beaufort is already within sight, we should be there 'fore noon."

"Thank you, Jonas, that's great news." He smiled, gave me a short bow, and left. If it was such great news, why did I suddenly feel a wreck of nerves. I wasn't expecting us to make landfall until late in the evening, possibly not until tomorrow.

And now I felt grossly unprepared. But grossly unprepared for what? I should be excited and relieved to be making it safely back to family. *This is what I'd damn near got myself killed for, after all.*

Maybe I was just nervous because this was a big deal. *Yes, yes, that was it.* I must be confusing my excitement and anticipation with nervousness.

Well, no matter either way. I would be walking off the ship in a few hours whether I was ready or not.

I noticed my father on the dock right away. He was wearing his kilt. The tartan fluttered proudly in the wind. He was ready for whatever was walking off this ship. He meant business.

I understood my father was already an intimidating man, but in his traditional highlander wear, he looked fierce—and I knew that was his intention too.

Elliot was standing a modest few feet away from me, but still reached across to give my hand a squeeze. I hadn't realized it had been shaking until he steadied it.

"Ye did it, Sloane," he said. "Ye ran away in the middle of the night—like a damn lunatic, I might add,"—that warranted a small chuckle from me, he sounded just like Abigail—"to get back what was yers, and ye've done just that."

l turned away from the banister to face him. I wanted to lean against his chest and have his strong arms wrapped tightly around me. But I knew we were within eyesight of my parents, so refrained.

"Ye survived being stolen, beaten, threatened and ravaged by one terribly handsome pirate." He winked.

"Bloody pirate." I rolled my eyes but couldn't deny that I felt a bit lighter now and ready to face my parents. I could do anything as long as I had my captain by my side.

After two men disembarked to set up the gangplank, I was the first to walk onto the dock. My father greeted me stoically while my mother staggered forward nearly in hysterics to embrace me in a tight hug. I was a little taken aback by her uncharacteristic display of emotion but was touched all the same.

"Ye nearly killed yer Ma running away like ye did, but I knew ye'd be back." I thought I caught a slight crack in my father's voice. "I'm happy to see ye but don't think I'm not mad as hell." He hooked one arm around me and pulled me close, hugging me like he thought he'd never see me again. Quite honestly, he probably did think that before he got my letter.

"I'm so proud of ye, my girl," he whispered in my ear as he squeezed me tight. This time there was no mistaking the distinct wobble in his voice as he crushed back tears, and I had to fight back my own.

He finally let me go, straightening his plaid and clearing his throat. I stepped back as well to make some room on the crowded dock for Elliot who stood behind me.

"Father, Mother, I'd like to introduce you to Captain Elliot Cross, he rescued me from the mutineers and took back possession of our wine." My two worlds were colliding, and anxious seconds passed before my father spoke.

"Well, sounds like we have much to thank ye for, Captain."

"It was my honor to be of service, sir." Elliot bowed and offered his hand to my mother. He held her fingers and dipped again in bow. "Yer humble servant, my lady."

My father puffed out his chest, assessing Elliot. I could tell that he initially approved of the man but sensed something was off that he didn't seem able to put his finger on. He'd always failed miserably at concealing his thoughts on his face.

"Come," my father said, "Let the men handle the unloading, no doubt we ha'e much to catch up on." He eyed me warily and I did my best to smile innocently. *So far so good.*

We sat gathered in the Dogwood Inn, uneasiness biting at me being back. I hadn't seen Margaret yet and didn't know if I wanted to. My father had believed her when she insisted she had nothing to do with my kidnapping and, while I wanted to believe him, I couldn't help but feel reserved.

Elliot sat across from me, next to my father. A purposeful distance set by my father no doubt. Even out of his domain, the ship, Elliot looked confident and at ease. He leaned back relaxed in the chair but kept his chest and chin up to not appear slouched or informal.

My mother seemed equally intimidated and smitten by him. She wasn't one to be shaken easily, but she seemed unable to meet Elliot's eyes. I didn't blame her, looking into his eyes was like staring into the universe. There was something so impenetrably far away but intimately close, like he could see your bare soul. Granted, I also had the added feeling that he was undressing me with his eyes whenever we were in public.

But overall, she did seem to like him, which was a wash of relief for me. He wasn't dressed in quaffed wigs and fine embroidered vests like Lord Thomas. He didn't speak with an upturned nose and flaunt his wealth at every opportunity either. I had half expected her to treat Elliot like the help and thought winning her over would be the harder task of the two.

"My dear Sloane!" A shriek came from the door, and I barely had time to register who it'd come from before I was swept off my chair, hands gripping my arms painfully tight, and a slobbering mouth mashed to mine. *Lord Thomas.*

I thrashed in his clutch, trying to escape his brutish advances. I heard chairs being aggressively pushed back, scraping across the floor, as everyone at the table abruptly stood.

It was only mere seconds but felt like hours as I struggled to tell him off with his tongue forcing its way into my mouth. My hands pinned to my body with a strength I didn't think him capable of, kept me from pushing him off me.

In a rapid blur of movement, Lord Thomas went flying, crashing into the nearest wall. Paintings shook and rattled to the floor. With lethal speed, Elliot was at his throat. Lord Thomas's eyes widened in horror as Elliot's blade bit into his skin. Elliot had him pressed violently up against the wall, his other arm like a bar across his chest.

"If ye lay a finger on her again, I'll cut it off." Elliot punctuated the seriousness of his intent by pressing the knife harder against Lord Thomas's throat. "If ye live long enough to try, 'cause I've a mind to slit yer throat from ear to ear right now," Elliot growled with such conviction I half expected him to follow through.

A sweet and pungent smell wafted past, and I noticed with mixed alarm and cruel satisfaction that Lord Thomas had pissed himself, a trail of darkened, wet fabric appearing down his breeches.

"Alas, I always give those I intend to board a chance to surrender first, so I suppose I can offer scum like ye the same." I felt my father still beside me as the realization of what Elliot was dawned on him. *Lord have mercy.* "So, what do ye say? Do ye accept my terms of surrender and promise to nay lay a hand on Sloane Sinclair ever again?"

Lord Thomas bumbled incoherent words and began to stumble away before I had a chance to knee him in the family jewels as I would have liked. He went scampering out the door, clutching his neck. *Oh please,* always a penchant for the dramatic. It's not like his neck was gushing with blood, Elliot barely broke the skin.

Elliot turned to me, his stormy gaze thick with lust. It was a look I recognized well by now. With his blood up from another man daring to touch me, I could tell he burned with the need to have me, to claim me, make it clear to everyone just who I belonged to. And if it weren't for my parents being present, I probably would have let him.

"Ye alright, lass?" He stopped himself from stepping any closer to me, his fiery gaze seeming to simmer down a bit. I still felt hot all over and could do nothing more than nod. *What I wouldn't do for him to bend me over a table right now.*

"Sloane." My father's gruff voice cut through the tension. "Outside, *now.*" His tone left little room for debate.

"A pirate! A damn bloody *pirate!*" My father kicked gravel, his face beet red. "How dare ye bring such a man into our lives!"

However angry he was, I can guarantee I was ten times angrier. Venom laced my words. "You speak of something you know nothing about! Elliot is a fine man who would give his life and body to protect me if called for. Isn't that what you've always wanted? A man you could trust to keep me safe when you're gone? To respect and care for me?"

"He's a monster, Sloane! They all are! How can ye no' see that?"

"Oh, you've spent the last month living with them, have you? Curious, I didn't see you the whole time *I* was on that bloody ship."

"He attacked Lord Thomas like a rabid dog. A damn brute is what he is!"

"As if you wouldn't have done the exact same! If Elliot hadn't threatened to cut off his hand for the way he forced himself on me, you surely would." I knew he couldn't deny I was right about that. I could practically feel the steam of rage coming of him in the inn.

"Ye're being a foolish *woman*." It was like all the blood drained instantly from my face with that one word. He knew exactly what to say to make it hurt. I went from seeing red to seeing blurry with tears.

"This *woman*, would be raped, ransomed and probably murdered if it weren't for that man." He paused his furious pacing at that. "Is that really what you'd prefer over me loving a pirate? My abused and violated body at the bottom of the ocean, huh? You'd rather that?" I demanded of him.

"*Love*? Ye canna love him, lass." I hadn't even realized I'd professed such a thing until he reiterated it. But as shocking as it was, it was true. I did love him.

"Men like him—"

"There are no men like him," I cut him off. He didn't speak, just stared at me lips pursed, jaw clenched.

"He sees in me the strong woman you raised me to be. He's a leader, a protector, a provider, just like you. He holds honor and family above all else. And while his family may be a ragtag group of misfits, he leads them with all his heart."

"Sloane—"

"No, let me finish. If you have any trust in my mind and my heart, you'll believe me when I say: you will not find a better man than Captain Elliot Cross." I walked off, leaving my father in the alley next to the Dogwood Inn.

I couldn't continue this conversation, if you could even call it that. My heart pounded and a lead weight sunk in my stomach. I'd never argued so vehemently with my father and over something so close to my heart. I just needed a break, some time to cool off to rationally approach the issue. And he needed the same. He needed to think about what he believed to be true and what his daughter *knew* to be true.

My father had always trusted my decisions. I just hoped he would trust me on this too.

• • •

Back in my room at the inn, I watched the storm clouds brewing outside the window. The door creaked open in time with a flash of lightning, and I jumped.

"Beg yer forgiveness, I didna mean to scare ye."

Margaret hesitantly entered the room, and I noticed my breath staying surprisingly steady. I guess my body had enough fighting for the day.

"I've already spoke with yer father, but I wanted to have words with ye too." She fretted with the hem of her shawl.

"I'm not mad, Margaret, it doesn't make any sense that you'd betray me." She visibly exhaled at my admission. "And trust me, I thought about it a lot." All the tension from the day on top of remembering the heartache I felt when I thought she gave me up made my eyes well with tears. *Was I really over it?*

"Oh, my sweet." My tears triggered the mother within her, she drew me into an embrace, all her anxiousness being replaced with maternal instinct.

I released a choked sob and felt every scared, angry and pained emotion from the last weeks pour through me. Margaret held me with a firm grip for such a dainty woman. The strength of a mother. The same strength that made women able to swim against a raging current to save their sinking child.

I'm sure part of me was believing what I wanted to believe but feeling Margaret's heart as she consoled me, I struggled to imagine she could ever do what I thought she had. I was exhausted and didn't have energy to waste on grudges and hurt.

"I canna fathom what ye've been through, lass." She rubbed a heavy palm in soothing circles on my back. "Thinkin' someone so close to ye turning yeh over to those devils."

"But if it wasn't you, how did they know?" My sobs had finally eased.

"A mousey lil' thing he was." She offered me her handkerchief. "I caught him sneakin' 'round the rented rooms, pockets full of bits and bobs, aye."

"Who?" I wasn't quite following.

"A mate on that blasted ship. Not long after ye left, I caught him but nay 'fore he snuck into just 'bout every place he shouldna. He was stealthy as a fox. He must've overheard us without being noticed, I figure."

Margaret had said the inn would creak at the drop of a pin, but I suppose that didn't totally eliminate the possibility that a particularly light-footed pickpocket could eavesdrop undetected. Having another possible suspect helped with forgiving her, if there was even something to forgive her for.

"Well, no matter now." I straightened my gown and wiped my drying tears. "I'm home safe, mission accomplished." I forced a smile but didn't fool Margaret.

"I don't know all ye've been through, but even if the end outcome is as ye'd like, it doesna mean the journey doesna still hurt."

"No, I'm good, truly."

"Ye're a strong lass, Sloane. No one's doubting that. But ye've been through a trauma and that takes healin', even for the strongest of us. Taking time to heal doesna make ye weak, only stronger. Remember that, aye?"

A few months ago, I wouldn't have given any weight to her words, but now I knew there was truth to what she said. Being strong didn't mean never having a weakness but being able to own that weakness without letting it define you.

CHAPTER FIFTEEN

Stupid Men

I didn't see Elliot after the incident with Lord Thomas and fell asleep alone, figuring he'd come to bed once the tavern had emptied. I assumed he was keeping busy out of sight.

But when I woke and he still wasn't beside me, the panic set in. *What if someone had told the redcoats he was a pirate?* It was no secret the Crown sought to make an example of anyone accused of piracy.

He could have passed as any other sailor if he hadn't blown up in a room full of people. *Damn him, if he got himself arrested, I swear to God...*

I debated rushing downstairs in my shift but decided against it. If he was in custody already, the extra minutes it took to dress wouldn't change anything.

Once downstairs, I took the backdoor out, not wanting to deal with the morning meal crowd. I made a beeline to the dock.

The crew was already bustling around, Jonas walked down the gangplank with big barrels on either shoulder—barrels that typically took two men to carry. What the man lacked in intelligence, he surely made up for in brute strength. He saw me and smiled.

"Ye lookin' for Cap'n, Mistress? "

"Yes, you know where he is?"

"In his cabin, m'um" *Not behind bars, that was good.*

Someone was repairing the deck right above the captain's quarters, so he didn't hear me come in. He was hunched over the desk, maps unfurled, his brow knitted with concentration.

I watched him for a moment. His sleeves were rolled up to the elbow and his forearms were taut with muscles as he pushed down on the desk. Who knew that when you find your person, something as ubiquitous as forearms could be beautiful?

Whatever he was looking at, apparently wasn't going how he wanted, he scowled at the parchments. He aggressively shoved the mess of rolls off his desk and fell back into his chair, running a frustrated hand through his hair.

"What did those rolls ever do to you?" His eyes shot up when I spoke and his tensed face relaxed when he saw me. But only for a second before turning hard and cold.

"What are ye doing here?" His tone was flat but harsh and took me by surprise. Not the greeting I was expecting.

"Looking for you." I glowered back, not knowing what was causing this bitterness. Surely he wasn't mad at *me* for

Lord Thomas's actions yesterday. "But apparently you don't want to be found." I huffed and turned to leave.

"Sloane, wait." He stood and circled the desk. "I'm sorry for my tone, aye." He reached out for my hand and pulled me to him, leaning against the desk.

"Let's try again, shall we? How was yer morn?" He wrapped his arms around me, and I was immediately comforted by the pressure.

"Well, I woke up thinking you'd been arrested, so it's going much better now I see that is not the case."

"Arrested? Why would ye think that?"

"When I realized you never came to bed, my mind jumped to the worst-case scenario, I suppose." Saying it out loud, it did seem a little dramatic of a conclusion. And to think that Lord Thomas would have enough courage to risk angering Elliot again after he made him wet himself was laughable.

My stomach growled audibly. He kissed my forehead. "Seeing as I'm no' arrested, how 'bout ye go fetch yerself a bite."

"Mm, that's a good idea." I pressed my lips to his and warmed. I could easily forget about my empty stomach if he kept kissing me like this.

Unlike our typical feverish and desperate kisses, these were slow and tender. Sensually pulling on my lip, delicate flicks of his tongue. They were sweet kisses, fueled by a love that was beyond primal lust.

The way his mouth melted into mine was as if he wanted to know me, not just have me. To know my heart and soul, not just share my bodily pleasures.

He pulled apart. "You've never kissed me like that before," I said breathlessly, even feeling a bit light-headed and not because I was needing food.

"I will always be grateful for ye, Sloane. Know that. No matter what happens, know that I will always carry ye in my heart."

"I know." Even though he'd never said those words before, I still knew. He held my gaze and the depths of his eyes seemed as vast as the ocean they were the color of.

• • •

"Where's Baby-Hands?" I asked my father who had just sat down at my table in the Dogwood tavern.

"Good morn to ye too," he said as he pulled a plate of ham across the table.

"I need to speak to the two of you."

"Aye, well he's probably too embarrassed to show face after pissing his breeks." My father stifled a laugh, and I couldn't help from cracking with a slight smile, despite still being angry with him.

"Why did you bring him anyway? I told you in the letter I had the wine, so there's no need for our engagement."

"He insisted." He tore a piece of bread. "And, of course, your mother loved the romantic notion of it all."

"Of course, she did," I groaned. She was probably hoping he'd sweep me off my feet. *Well, that certainly didn't happen.*

As if our conversation had summoned him, Lord Thomas waltzed through the inn door. He walked with his head held high, so high in fact that he wouldn't have to make eye contact with any of the patrons. His stock was wrapped several more times than customary to hide the cut on his neck.

"Sir." He bowed to my father. "My lady. I've come to apologize for my ghastly behavior yesterday." My father nodded, giving him permission to sit.

"I may consider granting you my forgiveness," I started, his unexpected apology actually could work to my advantage. "If you promise not to alert the authorities to Captain Cross's, hmm...let's say pastimes." Lord Thomas tensed at the mention of the captain and my father eyed him wryly.

"You too, Da." His head swung around shocked. "You don't have to like him, but you cannot turn him in. For my sake." Now it was his turn to tense up.

"Do I have your word?" My father seemed to weigh the benefits of turning him in versus royally pissing me off and quickly agreed.

"Aye, ye have my word." We both looked at Lord Thomas expectantly.

He forced a polite grin and spoke through gritted teeth, "For a chance to earn your forgiveness, you have my world as gentleman *and a lord*." Now I had to actively refrain from rolling my eyes, any excuse to mention his lordship.

"Good." I stabbed a sausage with my knife much harder than called for. "Then I accept your apology." I locked my eyes with his before chomping down on the sausage to which he winced, and I smiled.

That evening, I packed a basket of biscuit, cheese and apple for Elliot, who still hadn't left the ship all day. He must be making preparations for converting his crew from pirates to importers.

He wasn't in the captain's quarters when I arrived, but the desk was back to being littered with parchment rolls.

Curious and with nothing else to do, I wandered over to check out what he'd been so intent on. Perhaps navigating the best routes to pick up wine at different ports along the French Coast?

What I found was a route but not to France or anywhere in the Old World for that matter. It was trade routes in the West Indies with scribbled notes of what I assumed was their cargo—tobacco, cotton, sugar. And next to that, quick calculations for approximate price per share.

I read it over multiple times in disbelief at what I was reading.

He was planning another prize hunt.

My hands knotted at my side as I tried to calm myself. There must be an explanation. He was excited about going straight, I knew he wanted more for his men than the life of criminals.

Maybe he was just sorting through old papers so he could get rid of anything that might incriminate him.

Not able to fully convince myself, I rushed out of the cabin to speak with him immediately. I flung the door open and collided into him.

"Well, hello there." He steadied me.

"Why do you have the route of a prize ship out on your desk?" I shook off his grip and put my hands on my hips. The hallway was dark, but I could still see a flash of realization cross his face. He knew I knew. He definitely hadn't been sorting through clutter.

"I'm a pirate, Sloane, no' a merchant."

"You're a captain—what does it matter how you get your cargo?"

"I've been living this life for too long to ever go back. It's all my men know."

"But you can change!" I bit my lip to stop it from quivering. "You said you wanted that."

He took a heavy breath and averted his eyes before bringing them squarely back on mine.

"I said what I needed to, to get ye on yer back." It felt like the wind was knocked out of me, his words were impossible. "I'm a bloody pirate, lass. I take what I want when I want, ye said it yerself. Ye were just another plunder."

"Stop it." It came out as a whispered plea.

Why was he being so cruel? Every damn thought and expectation I had for pirates that he proved wrong came flooding back. Was my father right? Was I a fool for not seeing the monster that never left, but just got better disguised?

No, I refused to believe it.

"Stop lying," I spoke louder now, fury boiling up inside me. "You can lie to yourself, but don't you dare lie to me. If all you wanted was to get under my skirt, you would have the first night. I was easy prey locked in a bloody cage. But you didn't."

I could see pain flitter across his face; what I was saying was resonating with him.

"You can be scared, you can be unsure, but don't take the cowardly way out and push me away." I stepped up to him, so our chests were almost touching. I was calling his bluff and wanted him to see I wasn't backing down.

"I'm no' the man ye think me to be."

"Bullshit."

He shoved me, hard, against the wall and his fist closed around my throat. "Ye'd be wise to keep yer filthy mouth shut, lass."

I couldn't lie that I was scared. His fingers started to squeeze, my body was immobilized under the weight of his, but I didn't believe he would actually hurt me.

"Forget about me, forget about us, forget about any of yer foolish dreams of a future together. I'm telling ye now, they are nothing but that. Foolish dreams."

I forced myself to keep my breathing despite the pressure around my throat and my heart rapidly pounding in my chest.

"I shoulda let McDonald have ye, then maybe ye wouldna be so disillusioned that I actually care about ye."

Anger like I'd never felt before raged through me. Whatever his goal was with this act, that was too *fucking* far.

I spit in his face, and he stepped back, releasing me.

"I don't know what your goddamn problem is, but it's not my issue anymore," I shouted over my shoulder as I stormed away.

• • •

I tried to take comfort in the walk across the field to the stables like I used to, but I couldn't. Instead, the clang of bird chatter and dew soaking my boots just made me angry.

Everything seemed to make me angry lately.

It had been two nights since my parents and I had returned home. My heart felt brutally raw.

I wasn't dumb, I knew Elliot was purposefully pushing me away, saying things he didn't mean. But why?

That's what frustrated me the most. I didn't believe he would feel threatened in any way by Lord Piss-Himself. In fact, why would he even make such a scene defending me if he was planning on leaving me?

"It doesn't make any sense, Gerty." Gerty bucked her nose into my pet. "Especially what he had said earlier that day. He told me I'd always be in his heart. No matter what happened..." I froze, realization hitting me. *He'd known.*

He'd known then that he wasn't going to stay.

Tears pricked my eyes and Gerty gently whinnied, resting her head on my shoulder. I kissed her velvety nose. "At least I got you." She neighed in agreement.

I kept imagining him riding up to my house, telling me he made a terrible mistake and begging me to take him back. I couldn't even tell Gerty this little fantasy. It was so pitifully desperate. *I'm not some damsel in distress, and he sure as hell isn't my white knight.*

I forced myself to go through the motions of daily life so I wouldn't spend all day crying in bed—even if that's exactly what I wanted to do.

Losing Elliot, especially in such a confusing way caused such a deep hollowness it was hard to explain.

I'd thought I'd finally found my person, my partner.

I saw Abigail out the window and put the book I was failing to read down to meet her.

Abigail immediately drew me in for a bear hug.

"Don't you dare do something like that again, you mad woman." She stepped back but still held my hands. Her face was a wash of relief, joy and grief all at the same time. "I swear, Sloane, if you didn't come back, I would've never forgiven myself for letting you leave that night."

"It's good to see you too, Abby." I gave her hands a squeeze before sitting down in one of the rocking chairs. She sat in the other one.

"And don't be so hard on yourself. You know there was no stopping me, save physically restraining me, and with Malcolm bedridden there was no way you were doing that." She only scoffed in agreement.

"Speaking of, how is Malcolm?"

"A pain in my arse is what he is! In the house day and night, driving me mad." Abigail loved her husband, but also loved her personal time. I could only imagine her irritation stuck with him in their small cottage while he recovered.

"Though, I'm sure as soon as he's back on the road, I'll miss him sorely. Love is funny that way. You can be angry as the devil one minute and doe-eyed with affection the next." I laughed at the painfully accurate truth to that.

How many times had I been so boiling with rage I thought I might actually kill Elliot? But in the same breath also wanted to rip his clothes off. I guess that's why people called it madly in love.

"What happened out there, Sloane?" Abby's tone turned more serious, and I could tell she was dying to know but didn't want to push me.

"It feels like a lifetime ago." My mind wandered back to the alley with the crying baby. "The mutineers had found out I was going to tell the colonel the truth about the wine and laid a trap to steal me before I could follow through." I told her everything, starting from the alley in Beaufort all the way up to Elliot's absurd determination to return to piracy.

"This captain seems quite the fool."

"I wish I could hate him, I mean don't get me wrong, sometimes I think I do hate him, but I hate that he's not here with me even more."

"Love is exhausting, but it's not finite," Abby said." You may feel so tired you think you've used up all the love you have. But you haven't, Sloane. Your story isn't over yet."

"They leave that part out of all the fairy tales."

"Are you expecting any company?" Abigail asked out of the blue. I followed her gaze to the road leading to our house.

A horse was barreling toward us. Two riders perched on top, one so large that the second one was barely noticeable. I squinted into the sun, but they were too far away to make out who they were.

The rider's hulking form and break-neck speed was intimidating enough for me to send Abby into the house to fetch my father.

My father always kept a rifle under his rocking chair. I pulled it out and checked the priming. As the horsemen got closer, I realized I couldn't make out their faces because they were shrouded under cloak hoods. *Terrific, a pair of robbers was just what I needed on top of everything else.*

I raised the rifle and balanced the muzzle on the porch railing and crouched behind the sight.

"Make yourself known or I'll blow you off your damn horse." Actually, maybe this was exactly what I needed, an excuse to get all my anger out.

"I promise I'll shoot and enjoy it," I shouted again.

"I'm sure ye would Mistress Sloane, but I'd rather ye didna," That voice. I knew it.

He threw off his hood as he neared the porch and the mop of curly blond hair now visible made me laugh.

"Jonas, you devil, what are you doing riding up like a bloody bandit?

"Come lookin' for ye, Mistress," the smaller figure said, dropping his hood and Fish smiled back.

The very next moment, my father came bursting through the door, pistol raised.

"Who are the lucky bastards I get to shoot today?" he bellowed. Fish's hands shot into the air, but Jonas instinctually dropped his to the sword at his hip. My father saw the movement too and narrowed his sights on Jonas.

"Da, no!" I knocked the barrel of his gun off target. "They're friends," I said, exasperated.

"I see where ye get it from, Mistress." Jonas chuckled dryly as he dismounted and lifted Fish down.

"Sloane, who are these men?" my father said gruffly, still not convinced they meant no harm.

"The captain's second and..." I looked at Fish, who looked both startled half to death and beyond excited to see me. "And well, that's Fish."

My father didn't seem very relieved to hear they were part of the pirate crew and his fingers tightened on his gun again.

"And?" he prompted, eyes narrowed on Jonas.

"And we need yer help sir," Jonas addressed my father directly. "The Cap'n's been arrested."

• • •

"This is absurd. He delivered the wine back to us. Anyone on the dock that day would have seen the crew unloading the barrels." I rubbed my temples, unable to think clearly knowing the punishment for such grand theft was death.

"It was that weasel who soiled himself, m'um." *Lord Thomas.* "I did see him with the red coats, lookin' verra pleased with himself too."

"Blasted coward." Everyone's head turned at my father's surprising vitriol in defense of the captain. "Aye, I'm no fan o' the captain, but Lord Thomas broke his word and that's something I know the captain would ne'er do." I didn't bother questioning how my father knew that. I was too relieved knowing I'd have my father behind us for whatever we were going to do.

"If the weasel got us into this, he can get us out of it," I said decidedly and wasted no time heading straight out the door to Gerty.

I pounded on the door of the Thomas Estate's big house. The sound ricocheted into the house. I could also hear the crunch of hooves on gravel behind me as the others rode up.

"Lord Thomas, open this bloody door this very minute or I swear I'll burn the house down with you on it." Arson seemed like an appropriate threat given an inferno of rage had taken residence inside me.

Finally, I heard the lock click and I didn't wait for the door to be opened before pushing it open. I nearly knocked down the scared house slave who looked like she'd just let in a she-devil.

"Sloane, to what do I owe this pleasure of a surprise visit?" *Was he kidding me?* Acting cordial and oblivious after I'd nearly kicked his door in.

"You can drop the act, *lord*." The sickly-sweet smile faded from his face. "You're to ride with us to Beaufort today and recount your bogus accusation that the captain was the man who attacked the *Lilliana*."

"I will not." He sounded like an insolent child and my blood boiled. The others, Jonas, Fish, Abigail and my father, filed in, flanking me as I stared down Lord Thomas.

"Why do you care so much for worthless scum like him? I could give you the world, yet you choose *him* over me!"

"Have you ever considered that maybe *you're* the worthless scum?" I snarled and then a sharp whack filled the air. Lord Thomas's slap burned my cheek.

"You dare speak to me that way, you filthy pirate-loving whore." I only smiled back, knowing that any second the two men behind me would break his goddamn neck for hitting me.

Sure enough, my father swung a powerful uppercut into the lord's gut. Followed by my sweet, gallant Fish kicking him in the crotch while he was doubled over.

"My turn." Jonas smiled smugly before landing a punch that knocked the weasel out cold.

As soon as his body hit the floor my father was striding out the door. "We don't need him. I'll testify on the captain's behalf. It was my damn wine after all."

CHAPTER SIXTEEN

The Gallows

I sat at a table with my parents, Abigail and Jonas. My foot tapped repetitively making the table rattle. Margaret put a fresh pot of tea in the center of the table. She looked almost apologetic, like she wished she could be doing more than just providing refreshments.

Malcolm had a friend who worked in the magistrate's office, so he went to find out what he could about Elliot's case. When the Dogwood Inn's door opened, all eyes shot eagerly toward Malcolm.

"We're too late, he's already been sentenced. He hangs tomorrow." Malcolm looked pained as he delivered the news. My pulse went from anxious hammering to the stillness of death.

He hangs tomorrow.

Those three words gave me such a chill that I thought I might be sick. He hangs tomorrow.

Over my dead body.

Lord Thomas had asked why I chose Elliot. It's because there's a difference between giving someone the world and *being* their world.

And even though Elliot was acting like an idiot, I wouldn't let him swing. I refused to live in a world without him.

"That won't be happening." I stated simply.

• • •

Saving a condemned man on the day of his execution was no small task. But we'd spent all night brainstorming and had a solid plan. We just needed to get Elliot out of custody long enough for my father to convince the magistrate to issue a pardon. And hopefully not get anyone killed in the process.

Everyone, including the crew, was eager to help. Together, we might just be able to pull off the impossible.

A crowd had already begun to gather at the town center around the gallows. The sight of the towering wooden structure struck me harshly with the reality of the situation.

This was truly life or death. Luckily, I didn't have to face it alone.

I scanned the crowd from my saddle. I was positioned at the end of one of the four streets that led to the square. I spotted Fish winding through the crowd, leaving a trail of rope behind him. His small body easily squeezing in between people without them taking much notice. I looked to the roof tops and spotted the tops of the men's heads. They would be lying flat until it was time, just in case anyone looked up.

Although, everyone's eyes seemed to be fixed on either the gallows or the door of the magistrate's office, waiting for the prisoner to be walked out.

I didn't understand everyone's sick obsession in watching the execution of a man they didn't even know. If everything went to plan, they would get a very different show than they were expecting.

Jonas, Doc and three other crew mates were in the first row, stationed ready to jump into action. Though I hated the thought, I was comforted to see Doc there in case something went wrong, and we couldn't get to Elliot before he swung.

A fishy breeze blew past, making the emerald silk of my cloak wriggle like algae on rocks. In some random stroke of genius, I'd thought to pack it and had Abigail pack her matching one. I didn't know if or how they would come in handy at the time but thought having the ability to pass off someone else as me might prove useful. I felt like a big green light house in the thing, but that was the whole point after all, to be uniquely noticeable.

The crowd stirred and erupted into deafening cheers as Elliot was escorted out.

Seeing him was like a cannonball to the chest. His hands were tied behind his back and two soldiers held him by the arms.

He didn't look scared. Did he know we'd try to save him or was he just being brave? If anyone could face death with a cool expression of pride and content, it would be Captain Elliot Cross.

I wanted to scream and shout that I was here, that I was with him, that it would all be okay. Gerty sensed the energy from the crowd and shifted uneasily under me.

They marched Elliot up the steps to the gallows and my pulse quickened. Having to wait and watch him be prepared to be killed was nearly unbearable, but timing was important for our plan. We needed as few people on the gallows as possible.

At the moment, there were Elliot's two guards, a member of the magistrate's office, a priest and the executioner. The crowd, who had quieted after Elliot's entrance, now roared again as the magistrate's man read the charges against him and the verdict—Guilty.

The priest began to read Elliot his last rites and the two guards stepped to the back of the deck to make room for the executioner to place the noose around his neck. The taste of hot silver filled my mouth and I realized I'd been biting my inner cheek.

Now.

Where was Fish? Had he been able to set our plan in motion? The priest's voice droned on signaling time was running out to make our move.

Then there it was. I looked in the direction of a shrill scream and saw the licking flames. Fish had successfully lit the alcohol-soaked ropes he'd woven into the crowd.

Alcohol burned fast and hot and people scattered in alarm as a fiery snake raged among them.

People were running toward the streets that led out of the town square. As they clumped together trying to all fit through the narrow mouth of the streets, the men on the roof launched giant nets over them. The same nets used to board the broadside of a prize ship and big enough to trap the mob underneath.

Most of the redcoats had turned their attention immediately to the fire, which gave Jonas and his men opportunity to jump up onto the gallows and grab the remaining guards with a knife to the throat or a gun to the head.

They had very strict instructions not to kill or maim anyone. That would only make things worse for Elliot. That was one of the reasons we used the rope instead of grenades or lighting the gallows themselves on fire. The rope was low and confined and wouldn't spread from the wet ground. But was frightening enough to disperse the giant crowd.

It was my turn now. With my path cleared, I raced Gerty to the front of the gallows.

A mystified Elliot stared at me, and Jonas ordered the man he held at knife point to remove the noose from around Elliot's neck.

"Get on the horse, idiot," I shouted to spur Elliot into motion. He jumped onto Gerty's back behind me.

"Ye came," he said almost as a question, as if he didn't believe what was happening.

"Did you seriously think I'd let anyone beside myself kill you?" I could feel his chest rumble with laughter as he leaned against me to balance himself with his arms still tied behind his back.

The authorities had started to get their defense together after the initial shock of the attack had faded. A quick glance over my shoulder showed at least two red coats on horseback barreling toward us.

That's when I saw him. *Fish*.

His little body lay prone and still, I couldn't even tell if he was breathing. His face was swollen and battered, muddy footprints covered his clothes. He'd been trampled in all the chaos. I screamed his name, halting Gerty, but it elicited no response from him. Breathing became difficult and my heart felt like it was splintering into shards.

"I've killed him," I heard myself repeating over and over. I couldn't make myself move, my hands frozen on the reins.

"Go my lady, I've got him." Doc dropped to his knees at Fish's side. "Get yer man outta here. Go!"

A deafening shot rang out and a bullet whizzed past me. I heard the angry shouts from behind us and the hammering of horse hooves. Not needing another death on my conscience, I spurred Gerty into top speed.

Blinking rapidly to clear my vision of tears, I rode Gerty in and out of streets and alleys putting distance between us and our pursuers. I didn't want to lose them entirely, but needed enough time to make the switch.

I turned another corner, Elliot's body swayed dangerously close to toppling off the horse. I was on the same street as the Dogwood Inn. To my right was an alley that ran along the side of the inn. The redcoats still hadn't turned the corner yet giving us a small opportunity to dive into the alley where Abigail and Malcolm were waiting on horseback.

Abigail was wearing her bright green cloak and Malcom had a simple knit scarf thrown over his head to conceal his distinct red hair. We chose the scarf as it looked careless and unplanned, something seemingly thrown over Elliot's head as an afterthought.

As soon as we were out of sight and in the alley, Abby and Malcolm shot out and raced down the street I'd come down.

Me and Elliot dropped behind barrels just in time to see the red coats thunder past, now chasing the wrong pair.

I collapsed against the barrels, panting as much from adrenaline as exertion.

We'd done it.

Margaret burst out of the inn's backdoor. "Come, come, hurry." She shooed us inside and up the attic steps. The door to her secret room was already open and we rushed in. Even though I couldn't shake my last, lingering suspicions about Margaret—I'd spent weeks thinking she'd betrayed me, it was hard to turn that off—her secret room was our best chance of getting away with this crazy plan.

"My dear, only ye coulda pulled this off." She squeezed me in a quick hug before closing the door, locking me and Elliot in. Abigail and Malcolm weren't supposed to stop until a good distance out of town, but when they did and the authorities realized they'd been chasing the wrong horse, searches in town would begin immediately.

And we'd be hidden in plain sight.

Saving Elliot's life and then being locked inside a small, secret room with him wasn't as romantic as it might sound. Apparently almost losing someone entirely didn't wipe away all the hurt. I wished it was that simple.

But I couldn't bring myself to look at him, let alone speak to him. I sat pouting in the rocking chair, refusing to meet his gaze.

"Are ye at least gonna untie me?" He wiggled his tied wrists.

"No."

"Will ye talk to me, Sloane?" The ache in his voice was almost palpable, I nearly caved. "All I could think about when I was up there was that I was gonna die with ye thinkin' I didna love ye."

I was torn between wanting to scream and wanting him to hold me while I cried.

"Why would you say that? *You* left *me.*"

"And it was the hardest thing I've ever done."

"You're not being fair, Elliot." His words made me melt. I still wanted him so much it hurt and all I'd wanted was him to say the same. But he couldn't when it mattered most. And that wound was still fresh.

I didn't know if I could trust myself and my feelings around him anymore.

He opened his mouth as if to speak but nothing came out. There was understanding in his eyes. He knew he'd made a mistake in pushing me away and saying those awful things.

"Help me understand. Because dammit if I don't want to forgive you."

"I gave yer father my word." He looked at his feet like he was ashamed.

"My father?" That was not the answer I was expecting.

"He knows ye can do much better than me. He made me realize that if I truly loved ye, I wouldna force ye to be a criminal's wife. So, I gave him my word I wouldna make ye."

"Make me?" I stood and made him look up at me. "*Make me*? I don't know if you've noticed or not, but nobody makes me do anything I don't want to do." I poked him in the chest, "Not even you, *Captain*."

He stepped back and I matched it with a step forward. Part of me empathized with him because I know it must have torn him apart trying to make me hate him enough to leave. But this fool, in his misguided sense of love, tried to make a sacrifice that only ended up hurting me more.

I could feel his body tensing the closer I got to him, and I smiled inwardly knowing I still affected him. The back of his legs hit the trunk in the corner of the room and all it took was one small push to have him falling to sit on it.

I need him to feel what I felt. All the mixed emotions tumbling like sand in breaking waves.

"Do tell, what about me made you think I'd let a man make a decision about my life for me." It wasn't a question, it was a point. One I emphasized by straddling his lap.

I couldn't put into words everything I was feeling and thinking, so I would have to show him. I rocked slowly back and forth feeling him grow hard under me and watched with wicked fascination as his breathing deepened. With his hands still tied, I was in complete control, which gave me a heady rush.

I rucked up my skirt and continued to grind against his now bulging pants.

"Maybe I should take my pleasure like this, leaving you wanting, like you left me."

"If ye think I'll get no pleasure from ye ridin' me, ye're sorely mistaken, vixen."

The throaty groan he made from the next movement of my hips gave credibility to his claim. The apex of my thighs began to throb. My body needed him and the release only he could give me.

He leaned forward to drag his lips up my neck, planting a kiss under my jawline, then gently nipped the skin. "If I'm gonna hang today, I want ye to be my last meal," he whispered into my ear, sending chills down my spine.

It was a stark reminder that he hadn't been pardoned yet, that there might still be a chance the wall could come busting down and he'd be dragged back to the gallows.

I needed to have him, feel him inside me to reassure myself that he was still here and with me.

I hastily undid his pants and lowered myself onto him. We gasped in unison as he glided inside me.

I held his smoldering gaze, still not kissing him as I moved up and down his length, slow, teasing.

I let all the sensations of our closeness consume me. This was home. He was my home. I moaned with pleasure as I took in his eyes. Those eyes that had stirred something in me even the first time we met.

He bit his lip, trying to let me lead, not kissing me until I kissed him. He groaned and I smirked back.

"Ye're killing me, lass." His voice was strained with thinly veiled lust.

"Serves you right."

He matched my next stroke with a thrust of his own and I gasped at the deepness.

Suddenly his mouth was crushing against mine with frantic need and his fingers dug into my hips. *Wait, his fingers?*

Before I had time to register that he'd somehow undone his bindings, he was standing, clutching me to him.

He slammed us against the wall, one hand still cupping my bottom, the other palmed the wall behind me.

With one of my legs barely on the ground, the other wrapped around his waist, he pounded into me. His raw power made the tension coiled inside me grow tight and sweet. I rolled my head to the side, closing my eyes.

"Look at me." He tilted my chin to meet his heavy gaze. "I want ye to look me in the eyes when I promise I'll never leave ye again. I was a damn fool thinking I could ever live without ye."

Tears brimmed my eyes. His heart echoed mine.

• • •

Footsteps creaked on the ladder, the sound of feet following hands up the rungs. I shot up from where I'd been laying on the floor entangled with Elliot. He looked at me sleepily. "Did a mouse bite yer arse, my lady?" He rolled over and bit my hip.

"No, there's someone coming," I hissed in a whisper.

That had him jumping to his feet, quickly dressing himself as I straightened my own clothes.

He grabbed a candelabra and wielded it above his head. Feet padded across the front of the attic and stopped just on the other side of the false wall. Elliot stilled like a panther before it strikes as the wall began to open...

"God, it's you." I sighed immensely relieved to see my father and not militant red coats coming to fetch their prisoner.

"I'm no God, but I do come bearing good news," he laughed at his corny joke, holding out a sealed letter. "Ye've been officially cleared of all charges and pardoned, son."

"Thank ye, sir." He shook my father's hand but then my father pulled him into an embrace clapping him in the back. My jaw nearly hit the floor and Elliot looked equally surprised.

"Ye're a good man, a man o' yer word and that still means something to me." He looked at me, brows raised. "And my daughter seems to think yer good enough for her, so that's good enough for me."

"I did keep my word to ye, sir, but yer daughter had other plans." Elliot smiled at me, then pulled into his side with arm around my waist. "I'm sure ye know how that goes."

"Oh, I most certainly do," my father sighed with a matching grin.

"Da!"

"Dinna fash, my love, we wouldna have it any other way." Elliot kissed my temple and I thought, after everything that had happened, I might still get to have it all.

The End.

EPILOGUE

"What's next for you folks?" the gentleman asked both of us, but only made eye contact with Elliot.

"I'll have to defer to my wife for that one, she's the brains of the operation," he said proudly, and even after two years, I never tired of hearing him call me wife.

"We recently added two more ships to our fleet which will facilitate trade within the West Indies. Due to Elliot's past connections, we're able to safely travel along those routes without losing profits to pirates."

"How interesting." He had that bored yet intimidated facial expression most men got when speaking business with a woman. I didn't mind it much anymore. I no longer had anything to prove to anyone.

The man excused himself, mumbling something about champagne and Elliot placed a chaste kiss on my lips.

Even that seemed brazen for the Founder's Ball. The ballroom was filled with uncomfortable looking people engaged in overly animated conversations with fake laughter

I caught a glimpse of Jonas across the room, hilariously squeezed into a formal suit. He stood at the hors d'oeuvre table popping sausages rolls, one after the other, into his mouth, oblivious to the cluster of women eyeing him with curious affection, giggling among each other.

"He could have his pick of women if he ever noticed them," Elliot laughed beside me. "What do ye say we sneak out back and find a dark little corner somewhere?" Elliot whispered into my ear sending goosebumps down my arms. The tickle of his breath never failed to light me on fire.

"What do you say we simply head home and take our time in our own bed?" I yawned, poorly concealing it.

"Och, where's the fun in that?"

"I promise I can make it plenty fun." I heard a shocked gasp and realized another couple was within earshot. *Oops.*

"I suppose that's our cue, before someone has ye arrested for lewd behavior and public indecency." Laughing, Elliot took my hand, leaving Jonas to his flock of women and pastries, and the eavesdroppers to gossip.

The cold night air felt amazing on my skin after being in the hot ballroom packed with people. The pleasant sound of horse hooves filled the quiet streets as Elliot and I rode home.

Passing the warehouse, I smiled at the new paint job— *Sinclair Cross Trading Co.*

"I think they did a fine job," I said, warmed by seeing our family names painted boldly and proudly next to one another. We had been through so much but had accomplished even more together.

He was the partner I'd only dreamed of. I'd started to lose faith that a man like him even existed. Who knew all it took to find him was getting kidnapped and raided by pirates?

All the lights were out in the house except for one lone lantern left on in the foyer for us. As soon as we entered, I heard him snoring. He'd fallen asleep on the couch again. Not used to having a bed chamber of his own, he was still accustomed to falling asleep wherever he dropped.

I gently removed his blanket and folded it while Elliot scooped up his little body.

"Captain..." he said half-asleep before turning his head and lulling back to sleep. A scar curved around his eye and down his cheek. I could never look at it without recalling the horrifying image of him bloodied and trampled on the muddy ground, my brave little Fish. I ruffled his coppery hair which was still as much a bird's nest as ever despite my mother's best efforts.

While Elliot delivered Fish to his bed, I undressed in the candlelight, slipping into my night shift.

Elliot came up behind me and wrapped his arms around my waist, nuzzling into my hair, inhaling my scent.

He rubbed my round belly. "Lad or lassie, if they have even half yer strength and wit, we won't have much to fret about."

"Until they run off with some harebrained idea and get stolen at sea." I wrapped my arm up and around his neck, drawing him to me.

"We still have many years until that." He kissed my cheek and began to lift the hem of my shift. "But right now, you have a promise to keep, my lady..."

Dear reader,

Thank you so much for taking a chance on a new author. I hope you stick around for Jonas's love story in Stolen to Fight which will be released in early 2022 and can be pre-ordered on Amazon. Enjoy the book? You can make a big difference! If you have a moment, it would truly mean the world to me if you left a review on Amazon. Not just to fan my own ego, honest reviews are one of the best ways to support new indie authors and bring them to the attention of other readers. Even one-sentence reviews help! I would love to connect with you more personally, please join me on Facebook at Facebook.com/Groups/SummerOtoole for updates on future releases, advanced reader copies, to chat about our favorite books, or just to let me know that you're equally obsessed with Captain Cross.

Can't get enough of Sloane and Elliot? Sign up for my mailing list and I'll send you a bonus spicy scene right away...and maybe a sneak peek from Stolen to Fight too ;) This scene takes place within the timeline of the book during Sloane's return journey—enjoy!

I promise to send only periodic and relevant emails,
I hate a cluttered inbox too.
Sign up at SummerOtoole.com/StolenAtSeaBonus

ABOUT THE AUTHOR

SUMMER O'TOOLE has been writing books since she was eight years old, but *Stolen at Sea* is the first one she actually finished, making the fact that you're reading this the fulfillment of a lifelong dream.

She majored in Anthropology and Gender Studies at university which means she can tell you a lot about the history of human sacrifice, Bonobos' sex lives and theories for the evolutionary purpose of the female orgasm.

Having always loved anything romance, it only made sense to write epic love stories with swoon-worthy pirates and guaranteed happily-ever-afters.

ACKNOWLEDGEMENTS

An endless amount of gratitude to Best Friend Kelsey who has cheered me on every step of the way and my favorite member of our two-person book club.

This book would not have happened—or if it did, it would have been, quite frankly, terrible—without all the incredible coaching of Megan Yelle. You helped me get clear on the story I needed to tell and definitely shaped Sloane into the badass she is now.

To my MBA Accountability Babes who immediately recognized my dream and manifested it along with me.

Of course, none of this—or anything in my life—would be possible without the continuous support from my moms here on earth and my dad in heaven.

My brothers, for always rooting for me, putting up with me, and a "Ha, I win!" to my oldest brother who always wanted to write a book before twenty-five.

A big thanks to my beta readers for taking the time not only to read the roughest of rough drafts but to give thoughtful feedback too.

And to my editors, Saxony Gray and Marissa Taylor for making *Stolen at Sea* the best it could be despite my ongoing battle with commas.

Murphy Rae and Elaine York for bringing my vision to life and making *Stolen at Sea* something I can hold in my hands and be proud of.

Last, but absolutely not least, all my love and gratitude to my Gabby, who may not be able to fight like Captain Elliot Cross but loves just as fiercely.

Made in the USA
Middletown, DE
22 January 2022